Always Mine

The Barrington Billionaires

Book One

Ruth Cardello

Author Contact
website: RuthCardello.com
email: Minouri@aol.com
Facebook: Author Ruth Cardello
Twitter: RuthieCardello

When it comes to getting what he wants, Asher Barrington is a hammer who is known for crushing his opponents. From the moment Emily walks into his office and challenges him, winning takes on a whole new meaning.

The only thing standing between Emily Harris and her goal to open a museum for the blind is an arrogant, sexy as hell billionaire, who thinks sleeping with her will not complicate the situation.

He won't change. She won't back down.
But together they sizzle.

Be the first to hear about my releases
ruthcardello.com/signup

One random newsletter subscriber will be chosen every month in 2015. The chosen subscriber will receive a $100 eGift Card! Sign up today by clicking on the link above!

COPYRIGHT

Dedication

This book is dedicated to Jan, aka JS Scott. My writing journey has brought many wonderful people into my life; I love that you are one of them. You are one of the most giving people I have ever met, especially when people accidentally dine and dash. I hope just as much love comes back to you as you send out into the world. Your next drink is on me. Unless I have somewhere to go and forget to pay. . .then I'll catch the next one after that.

A Note to My Readers

Hate to say goodbye to your favorite characters? So do I, that's why the gang from the Legacy Collection and the Andrade series are back in the Barrington Billionaires. You'll love watching Dominic Corisi step in with his usual flair to save the day.

In this book, you will be introduced to Brice Henderson, Asher's business partner. Pick up the first book in Jeannette Winters' new series, ONE WHITE LIE. Not only do I love her writing, I love her. She is my sister, after all.

You'll also meet, James West, the son a business competitor. My billionaire world extends into a yet another series, this one by Danielle Stewart. Book one: FIERCE LOVE.

Three authors, three series, all able to be read independently, but intertwined as only a family could weave them. I write about large families and the love that brings them back together. Who better to partner with for a new billionaire world than my sister and my niece? While we may not be billionaires, we certainly understand the challenges of a large family and, more importantly, the real blessing that being part of one is.

Chapter One

ASHER BARRINGTON PUSHED a small package off to one side of his Boston office desk and stood. Distant relatives had recently become persistently, tediously interested in opening a dialogue. The package was their latest attempt and would hit the trash unopened. Asher had little time and even less patience for "family" who had done nothing when his parents had needed their support.

His mother's side, the Stanfields, and the Andrade family his Aunt Patrice had married into, were both extremely wealthy. Either of them could have come to the aid of his father and stopped him from losing his career, but they hadn't. Why? Because no one respects a weak man.

Asher had been old enough to be shamed by his father's scandal. When his classmates had heartlessly taunted him, Asher had discovered how very different he was from his father. He hadn't retreated from confrontation. He'd gone after those who'd found enjoyment in his pain and had taken them down with whatever means was at his disposal. He'd been smart enough to keep the evidence of his retaliation off the radar of the school and his parents. Except for the time he'd taken on a bully. He'd made sure that fight was both public and final. No one had laughed at him after that day, and that win helped shape the man he'd become.

He'd taken his trust fund from his grandfather and built a financial empire with it. Regardless of how successful he became, he had yet to hear his father say he was proud of him. When they did speak of his business his father would only caution him to soften his approach, tread more carefully, risk less. That wasn't how Asher operated nor was it how he wanted to. He had goals for himself and his company, and if that meant crushing his opposition, it was nothing more than the way of the world. Eat or be eaten. Expand or perish. Asher's father had been a great man, but he should have fought harder for what he had. Asher was determined to not make the same mistake.

Nothing and no one stood between him and a goal. When Asher had first started his biochemical company and then expanded it by undercutting the prices of the competition, his father had said, "Be careful. When you're a hammer, everything looks like a nail."

Asher had given up trying to explain how the world worked to his father. His parents were perfectly happy in their middle-class home, driving their ten-year-old cars. They certainly weren't poor, but they considered themselves better off for not having fought his mother's family for anything other than their children's trust funds. How a man who had once been one of the most influential US senators and a woman who'd been born into the top of the privileged one percent could be satisfied with obscurity was a constant mystery Asher had given up trying to solve. One of Asher's brothers, Lance, believed their mother had been afraid of her father as well as her sister. Both were dead now so that was another topic that held little interest for Asher. Had his mother ever appealed to him for help, Asher would have dealt with both of them for her. He feared no one.

There was a light knock on the door and Ryan Corson, Asher's personal assistant, entered. He was a reliable, unflappable, problem solver and that had made him an indispensible member of Asher's team. He was paid well above his job description because he had proven himself in a variety of ethically complex situations. Asher didn't need a conscience; he needed a team that would follow his orders without hesitation, so those were the people he'd surrounded himself with.

"Mr. Corisi is quickly becoming impatient," Ryan said. "Shall I send him in?"

Asher sat on the edge of his desk and checked his watch. "Tell him I'm on a conference call for five more minutes."

Ryan grimaced. "He may not wait."

"He will. He's curious."

"I'll tell him, but I'm guessing not too many people make Mr. Corisi wait for anything."

"Exactly," Asher said with a flash of teeth. Dominic was known for losing his temper easily. "Always play to your opponent's weaknesses."

Ryan gave Asher a curious look. "Is he our competition? He's in an entirely different industry."

Asher pushed off the desk. "Every person who is not on

my team is against it. Remember that. Dominic is getting impatient. Good. Keep your opponent off balance and it's easier to get information from them."

Ryan neither agreed nor disagreed. He retreated to his office and to the likely unpleasant task of informing one of the most powerful people in the country that he needed to cool his heels for a few more minutes.

Asher slowly checked the messages on his phone, straightened the already straight papers on his desk, and finally opened the door of his office. "Dominic, thank you for coming."

Dominic turned and gave him a dark look Asher pretended not to see. Dominic growled, "When you said it was a matter that couldn't be spoken about on the phone, you piqued my interest." Although Dominic didn't mention it, his irritation at being kept waiting was obvious. "This had better be important."

Asher smiled smoothly, deliberately ignoring that as well. "Come in. Ryan, hold my calls." He waited until he knew Dominic was paying attention and added, "Unless it's Freethy. Then put him through." He heard Dominic's impatient huff and hid his satisfaction at how easy it was to use a man's pride against him. After closing his office door, he said, "Have a seat, Dominic."

Dominic folded his arms across his chest and kept standing. "I don't have time for whatever game you're playing, Asher. What do you want to discuss?"

Asher rocked back on his heels and pocketed his hands in his trousers. "I need the name of your contact in Trundaie."

Dominic studied him for a long moment, then said, "I don't deal with unstable governments anymore."

Asher smiled knowingly. "I understand. You have a family to think about now."

"I do."

"How is your wife? And your daughter—Judy, isn't it?"

Dominic relaxed his stance. "Both are well. Judy just started kindergarten."

"Wow, that happened fast."

"It did. It feels like only yesterday I was learning to change a diaper. In a blink of an eye, she's reading to me at bedtime instead of the other way around."

Asher leaned back against his desk. "Tell me, how long do I have to pretend to give a shit about your family before you cough up your old contact in Trundaie?"

Dominic's eyes narrowed, then he barked out a laugh. "You remind me of myself, Asher, and that's not a compliment."

Asher picked up a folder, took out a photo of an outbuilding that had been destroyed, and threw it on the table near Dominic. "I'm having issues with the rebels in Trundaie. We both know they don't care why I'm there. This is extortion, plain and simple. I know they went against you when you were there, and you paid someone in the military to get them to back off. All I need is a name, and I'll handle the rest."

Dominic shook his head. "I told you, I've distanced myself from those contacts. Trundaie's instability has increased since I was last there. I understand the temptation of fast money that can be made in places no one else will go, but don't underestimate the price you pay for making those kinds of enemies."

With a sarcastic chuckle, Asher straightened. "How does it feel to be a lion on a leash? We've worked the same international circuit for too long for me to believe you don't still have your hand in it. The contract we have with Trundaie will open up the whole Asia continent to using our product. They pride themselves on their low prices, and using our synthetic material instead of oil will cut their production prices in half. We don't have to stay in Trundaie. The government will purchase our facility once we've proven to them that it can be lucrative. Once we have them, the Western markets will cave because they'll have no other choice. They'll need either a facility or product from us. Maybe you can't play in the big sandbox anymore, Dominic, but don't begrudge me the pleasure. All I need is a name."

Dominic shook his head, but said, "I'll make a call."

Asher crossed the room and held out his hand. "I'll send you a postcard from Trundaie."

Dominic shook his hand. He didn't look the least bit bothered by Asher's baiting. "You're wrong about one thing, Asher. I don't miss my old life. It was exciting, but it was empty. Life is about more than that."

Asher walked him to the door. "I'll take your word for that. Thanks for coming by."

Dominic nodded and added, "Coming by was never in question. Some of your family has become like my own."

"If you mean the Andrades, you can have them," Asher

said.

Dominic gave him an odd look but didn't say more before leaving.

After he was gone, Asher called his business partner, Brice Henderson. He didn't waste time with pleasantries. "I need you to move the deadline up."

"The compound needs an additional round of testing."

Brice was a genius, but he didn't understand the complexities of the volatile international market. "The sooner we have the facility up and running, the sooner we can hand it off to the government and get the hell out of there. Get me the product ahead of schedule."

"Nothing will happen if I can't get this compound right."

"'Nothing' is not an option. We're delivering something to them. We have too much riding on this not to. Do whatever it takes."

"Asher, unlike your Neanderthal negotiations, science cannot be rushed."

"Things are heating up in Trundaie. We need the standing government to back us, but they won't do that until we show them how profitable it will be for them. We need to get our facility up and running . . . now."

"It'll be ready by the date we agreed to."

Asher hung up the phone and retuned to his seat behind his desk. Arguing with Brice would be a waste of time. He rubbed a hand roughly over his face and typed in the password on his computer. His cell phone beeped, announcing a text. It was an encrypted message from Dominic. A name.

Perfect.

The phone on his desk buzzed. "Mr. Barrington, there is a Ms. Emily Harris here to see you. She said she has an appointment, but it's not on my calendar."

"I don't know the name. Tell her I'm in a meeting, and she'll have to come back, but don't schedule her."

Ryan lowered his voice. "I tried that, Mr. Barrington, but she said your mother made the appointment."

"Shit." He vaguely remembered agreeing to speak to someone. It was probably one of his mother's friends, older than sin, possibly senile, and most likely there to ask for a donation to some charity his mother thought he should care about. The quicker he met with her, the sooner she'd be out of his hair. "Send her in."

EMILY HARRIS CROSSED and uncrossed her legs nervously, then tucked a defiant curl back behind her ear. She looked down at her French manicure and took a deep, calming breath. The life expectancy of acrylic nails on her was less than a day. She'd purchased a beige dress suit for the trip, but it was her only business attire, so she hoped Mr. Barrington could be persuaded to change his mind in one meeting.

Emily wasn't normally a confrontational person. She was a self-professed people pleaser. To her, there was nothing wrong with wanting those around her to be happy. Both her grandfather and her mother had done everything they could to give her a good life. She was grateful, and that gratitude was the fuel that fed her determination to take her fight directly to the CEO of B&H Advanced Engineering. If anyone had told her six months ago she'd be in Boston taking on one of the nation's richest men, she wouldn't have believed herself capable.

But here I am. It's amazing how motivating a dose of desperation can be.

When B&H first began their attempts to purchase properties in her town, she hadn't worried. Her land was nearly dead center on the proposed plans for demolition and development, but she'd been confident her neighbors would never sell. One by one, though, they'd accepted offers and moved away.

At first, Emily had tried to reason with the company representatives who relentlessly offered to buy her land. When that didn't work, she stopped answering their phone calls. Their unopened letters were piled on her kitchen table. She hoped if she blocked all communication with them they would see how serious she was.

Their response had been a summons to court. It wasn't until she'd taken the letter to a lawyer and been advised to sell that she understood how dire her situation was.

"I won't sell," she'd told the lawyer.

"You won't have a choice," he'd answered sadly, removing his glasses and placing them on his desk. "I could cite countless similar cases where the plaintiff lost or took a payout in arbitration. Why put yourself through that? Make them an offer you can live with and move. You don't have the resources to win against a company like B&H."

"I won't sell," she growled before she gathered her papers and left the office of the only lawyer within fifty miles of her home.

I won't.

It didn't help her confidence when she heard Mr. Barrington's secretary admit he'd tried to get rid of her and failed.

After weeks of trying to contact Mr. Barrington and being given the runaround, Emily wasn't going anywhere until she was given a chance to speak to him in person. *I don't care how long I have to sit here. I didn't come this far to give up now.*

An office door opened. Emily stood quickly, dropping her small purse on the floor in front of her. Because the universe had a mischievous sense of humor, most of the contents spilled out onto the rug at her feet. She scrambled to pick everything up and groaned when she saw her wallet had bounced beneath the chair she'd been sitting on. She bent but couldn't reach it, so she went down onto her knees and grabbed it, stuffing it back into her bag before standing.

As she straightened she noted the polished pair of shoes standing less than a foot away. Her eyes scanned their way up a pair of charcoal trousers, a stark white shirt, and an expensive looking tie before landing on the face of the man the suit had obviously been tailored to fit. Her artistic eye missed nothing. Not the breadth of his chest, the strong lines of his jaw, nor the boldness of his hazel eyes. Mr. Barrington was not the soft suit she'd expected to meet after speaking to his mother. As much as the artist in her appreciated his symmetry, the woman in her was rocked back by the power emanating from him. Although they had yet to exchange a single word, Emily knew she was in the presence of a man who demanded instead of asked. She didn't want to be, but for just a second or two she basked in the desire that kind of masculinity sent tingling through her. She knew she should say something, but the exact reason for her meeting with him temporarily eluded her. One of her curls sprang free and fell across her face. She swayed and continued to take in the perfection of the man before her.

His smile was cold and that helped remind Emily why she was there. He held out a hand toward her as he gave her another head-to-toe evaluation. "Emily Harris. It's always a pleasure to meet one of my mother's friends."

Emily hesitated before placing her hand in his. Lying didn't come easily to her. "I'm not actually—" Emily started to admit then stopped herself. She could only imagine what he'd say if she said the truth. *I needed to talk to you, and you wouldn't see me, so I asked my hair stylist if she could help. She knew someone who knew the nanny of a woman who plays bridge with your mother. A few phone calls. More than a little begging and explaining why I had to speak with you, and here I am. Right here. Holding on to your hand and wondering what the hell I can say to make you care about my plight.* Emily pulled her hand free, squared her shoulders, and said, "Thank you for seeing me."

Emily spent a good deal of time studying the faces of strangers and honing her skill when it came to capturing their essence in the clay sculptures she created for a living. Although she was far from famous, her work brought her a steady income, and that was more than many artists could say. She searched the expression on the man before her. His face was carefully devoid of emotion. He was a man in control, even of himself.

He glanced at the wall behind Emily, then down at her again. "You have ten minutes of my time. Follow me." He walked back into his office without waiting to see if she would.

She met the eyes of the male assistant briefly. If she was hoping for some encouragement, there was none there. He looked away and started typing. Emily raised her chin and hoped she looked confident as she walked into what represented her first foray into the world of big business.

Mr. Barrington was sitting on the corner of his desk with his arms folded intimidatingly across his chest. "If you're coming in, close the door behind you."

"Sorry, of course," Emily said more apologetically than she meant to. *Damn it, I'm not sorry. I'm angry, and I have every right to be.* She walked over to the chairs just in front of his desk.

He looked at her for a long moment. "Have a seat."

Be strong. She swallowed hard and met his eyes again. "I'd rather stand."

A spark of something lit his eyes briefly before his expression became guarded again. "What are you doing here, Ms. Harris?"

Emily clasped her hands in front of her and said firmly, "I came to give you a warning."

His eyebrows rose ever so slightly in surprise, and a faint smile pulled at his lips. He lowered his hands to the desk on either side of him and leaned forward. "Really?" He glanced down at his watch. "This should be interesting."

What a self-centered bastard. Emily's back straightened with pride. *Laugh now, but you won't be amused when you realize how serious I am.* "You may think you won in Welchton, but you haven't. You don't have my land yet, and you won't get it. If you take me to court, I will win, no matter what your army of lawyers tell you."

Asher leaned back and pressed a button on the phone on his desk. "Ryan, are we buying property in Welchton?"

The assistant's voice came across on speakerphone. "Yes, sir. You wanted a northern New England research facility. We chose New Hampshire. You signed the paperwork to move forward with it."

"I did. How far along is the project?"

"We have all the permits. We're waiting to resolve one minor issue."

"Is that issue a reluctant seller?" Asher's eyes held Emily's as he spoke.

"Yes, but we don't foresee it being a problem for long."

"Nor do I," Asher said firmly. "Ryan, interesting fact about Ms. Harris. She's from Welchton." He hit the button on the phone again, ending the call. He rubbed his chin and studied Emily. "Let me guess: You feel your property is worth more than we offered."

There it was, the opening for her to explain the reason she refused to sell. She had to believe he was a reasonable man. Once he heard the history of the property and her plans for it, he'd surely change his mind about buying it.

"There is no amount that would convince me to sell. My family—"

He straightened to his full height and looked her over again. "No amount? How about double what they offered you?"

Emily clenched her hands at her sides. It wasn't what he said, but how he said it, that was insulting. "Do you know what their proposal was?"

"No."

Anger burned and grew within Emily. She took a deep breath, though, and told herself to remain calm. There was a chance he didn't know what he was about to destroy. "If you'd give me a minute to explain, I think you'd feel—"

Asher stepped closer to her, watching her expression closely. "How I feel is irrelevant when it comes to business." He stopped less than a foot in front of her, forcing Emily to crane her neck to look up at him. "Why don't we end this little game now? Tell me what you're holding out for, and I'll tell you if you have a chance in hell of getting it."

"This isn't a game. The Harris Tactile Museum is six months from completion. Maybe if you came up to see it, you'd understand how important it is."

He didn't look the least bit interested. "I'm sure our offer took your relocation cost into account. If not, counter with an amount that would, and my people will crunch the numbers."

"I'm not selling, Mr. Barrington. Period. I won't let you steal my land, and that's what you'd be doing, even if you did it in a court of law. Having enough money to buy the outcome you want doesn't make it right."

His smile was indulgent and Emily, who considered herself a non-violent woman, was tempted to smack it off his face. "I like your spirit, Ms. Harris, but that doesn't change that you're standing between me and something I want. If I were you, I'd put together a counterproposal you can live with. I'll give you my email. You can send it to me personally, and I'll make sure it's at least considered."

She leaned toward him and threatened, "I may not have money, but I care about this museum, and other people will, too. I won't be sending you a counteroffer, because I'm not selling."

A corner of his mouth curled in a way that sent waves of heat through Emily. "I always get what I want, Ms. Harris."

Emily stepped back. "Not this time." She walked out and closed the door firmly behind her, taking a brief moment to lean against it for support before pushing off. She defiantly moved her wayward curl off her face and held her head high as she walked past the desk of Asher Barrington's snooty assistant.

Chapter Two

I CAN'T BELIEVE I thought he'd care. What a pompous jackass. "I always get what I want." Well, not this time, buddy. My mother didn't let anything stop her from following her dreams, and I won't let someone like you stop me from building a tribute to her. As she drove out of Boston and into one of the surrounding suburbs, she rehashed her heated meeting with Mr. *I'll make sure it's at least considered* Barrington again and again. Jerk.

I should have kept my cool. I should have spoken more about my mother and the reason the museum needs to be where I'm building it.

Not that he probably would have cared. Bastard.

I was hoping to do this the easy way, but it looks like I have to go with plan B.

Obstacles are opportunities if you're brave enough to take them on. That was what her mother had always said. Emily refused to give up. Determination was in her genes just as surely as art was.

Her mother, Wendy Harris, had lived a life that had inspired everyone who knew her. Born blind, she hadn't let that stop her from becoming an artist, a painter at that. Her works were uniquely tactile. She'd pushed the limits of what was considered a painting and had developed a technique that brought a three-dimensional element to her artwork.

Emily's own appreciation for art had been acquired at her mother's knee. They'd spent countless afternoons in museums. Her mother would ask Emily to describe a painting, first with what she saw, but then with greater detail about how the painting made her feel. Eventually Emily began to use clay to make the paintings her mother loved even more accessible to her.

Her mother had dreamed of creating a museum where people could run their hands over every piece of artwork displayed. A place where those who could not see were not banned from experiencing masterpieces. Nothing would stop Emily from making that museum a reality.

Determination made it possible for Emily to consider the unthinkable. Plan B was bold and more than a little underhanded. To some degree she felt like a snitch, but she steeled herself against her doubts. She was desperate.

She hit redial on her phone. A woman answered. "Mrs. Barrington?"

"Emily? Do call me Sophie. Mrs. Barrington sounds like I'm one hundred years old." Sophie's next comment was directed to her husband, Dale. "It's the woman from New Hampshire who is building a museum." She paused as if listening to a response from her husband before saying, "Did you make it to Boston?"

"I did. I'm actually driving back to my hotel in Newton."

"That's only a town over from us."

I know. "What a coincidence," Emily said instead.

"My husband and I are just about to have lunch. If you have time, we'd love to meet you in person. You could tell us all about your meeting with our son."

"That sounds wonderful," Emily said with just the right amount of pleased surprise.

Emily pulled into a highway rest area and typed the address into her GPS. She told Sophie she'd be there in less than an hour. After hanging up, she stayed in her car, taking deep breaths and telling herself she was doing the right thing.

When her nerves had settled somewhat, she called her best friend for support. It rang through to voice mail the first time, but Emily called back. *Come on, Celeste. Pick up.*

When Celeste finally answered, she said, "I'm in a meeting with a client. Can we talk later?"

"This is an emergency."

"I need to take this call. Tim, could you take over for a minute? I'll be right back," Celeste said. A moment later, she asked, "Did you break down on the side of the road? Are you hurt?"

"My car is fine. I'm fine."

"Then what's the emergency? I'm meeting with a new client right now who has flown in from New York. This could be big, Em."

Emily instantly felt badly about interrupting her, but they'd been best friends since kindergarten and, although Celeste had moved to Boston after college, they'd kept that friendship close by staying involved in each other's lives.

"Remember how I told you I was going to go see Asher Barrington? I just left that meeting. It didn't go well. So, I'm moving onto Plan B."

"Wait, is that the crazy idea you had about befriending his parents and guilting him into moving his facility?"

"It's not crazy. Some people listen to their parents. It's worth a shot, anyway."

"Don't do this. I know a few lawyers. I'll call one tomorrow."

"I don't have money for a big-city lawyer. All my money is tied up in the museum. You know that."

Celeste sighed. "I could try to talk one of them into doing it pro bono."

Emily gripped the steering wheel tightly. "You think they'd take on B&H for free?"

Celeste made a frustrated sound. "No, probably not. You really went to see Asher Barrington?"

"Yes, and you would have been proud of me. I didn't let him intimidate me. I made it clear I wouldn't sell my land at any price."

"That must not have gone over well. What did he say?"

"He said he always gets what he wants."

"Oh, boy. And then?"

"I told him he wouldn't this time. And I walked out."

"And now you're off to meet his parents?"

Emily looked around at the parking lot she hadn't yet built up the nerve to leave. "It's the only way, Celeste. He doesn't care who he hurts or even about the facility he's building up there. He didn't even know how far along the project was. Maybe he won't care what his parents think either, but what other choice do I have? The museum is so close to being ready to open its doors. I can't let him take that from me, from everyone who would enjoy it."

"Em, this has trouble written all over it. I don't like it."

"That's not good. I was hoping you could give me one of your pep talks. I'm more nervous than I thought I'd be."

"That's because you know this is wrong. Emily, you don't have a manipulative bone in your body. You've never been a good liar. Oh my God, remember that time you accidentally walked out of a store with an extra item in your cart and almost got arrested because you had to return it and confess? Anyone else would have left it there or taken it with them and not thought twice about it, but you couldn't. It's part of what I love about you, but it's also why this will never work."

Emily put her car in drive and pulled back out onto the highway. "I can't be that person right now, Celeste. I have to be stronger than that. Tell me this can work. Even if you don't believe it. Just say it. I need to hear it."

After a long quiet moment, Celeste said, "If anyone can get someone's parents to love them, it's you, Emily. Just be careful. Yes, your mother wanted you to finish her dream, but your safety would have mattered to her more than any building ever could."

"I know what I'm doing."

"You're way out of your league, Em, and I'm saying this as a friend who loves you like a sister. You're not a fighter; you never have been. Do you remember when Donnie Allan tried to rough you up for your lunch money? I told you to punch him in the face. You sold brownies from the end of your driveway for a week to raise enough money so you could both have lunch."

"Yes, and it worked. I gave him the money, but I was firm that it was a one-time deal. He never bothered me again after that."

"That's because I threatened to tell everyone he wore his sister's underpants if he didn't leave you alone."

"Oh my God, you never said a word."

Celeste made a strangled sound. "You're a nice person, Em. There's nothing wrong with that. You like to believe there is good in everyone, but sometimes there isn't. Donnie was a bully. Your way doesn't win against that. I'm afraid nice won't win with B&H either. I wish I had the connections to help you with this, but I don't."

A lump of emotion clogged Emily's throat and made it difficult to get the next words out. "I don't have a Plan C. This is it. If I go home now, it's over. I'm doing this, Celeste. Even if it's the craziest idea you've ever heard, tell me it'll work. I need my best friend to believe in me right now."

In a tone that revealed how much Emily's plea had moved Celeste, she said, "You've got this, Emily. Call me after you win his family over."

AFTER A LONG jog along the Charles River, Asher took the elevator up to his penthouse apartment in Beacon Hill. He downed a glass of water and checked the messages on his phone while heading toward his bedroom. His mother had called but hadn't left a voice message.

He threw his phone on his bed and stripped. He'd shower, have something quick to eat, then deal with whatever manner of family crisis she wanted his help with this time. As the oldest of six children, there was always something.

He turned on the shower and stepped beneath the hot spray. Six children. If he'd ever doubted his parents' sanity, the number of children they'd decided to have was evidence enough they were both crazy. Five boys and one girl. He wasn't sure if his parents had stopped having children because they finally had a little girl, or if more hadn't been possible, but either way they had done more than their fair share in populating the planet.

Asher turned his back so the water massaged his shoulders. It had been a very long day, but he'd done what he'd set out to do. He'd made contact with the man Dominic had directed him to, and if all went as planned the rebels would have a nasty fight on their hands very soon. It was an expensive and dangerous course to take, but he'd been down that road in other countries and won. Being a hammer had its advantages. He won again and again because he'd built a reputation for smashing through whatever was in his way. In business, few people had the nerve to stand up to him and those who did were quickly, decisively, shown why they shouldn't attempt it again.

Everything would be a hell of a lot easier if he could apply the rules of business to his private life. Both his parents and siblings were as frustrating as trying to walk across a floor covered with marbles. He'd fought for a life where things made sense and he was in control, but he had no control over his family.

He lathered his hair and thought of something more pleasant than his impending conversation with his parents. A vivid image of the woman who had come to his office earlier that day filled his thoughts.

His first view had been her cute little ass waving in the air as she'd been on her knees digging for something beneath a chair. Her skirt had ridden up, revealing tight thighs he'd wanted to run a hand between. He closed his eyes and images of her brought a lusty smile to his face.

He had a healthy sexual appetite, and he'd found Emily Harris very attractive. She was a small thing, shorter than his usual taste. He pictured how easily it would be to lift her so she could wrap her legs around him as he thrust up into her.

There had been nothing suggestive about their meeting, but his cock hardened with anticipation as he replayed their exchange in his mind. Women didn't normally stand up to him, and she had done so fearlessly.

When she'd stood there, her eyes flashing and chest heaving, he'd found himself in the unique situation of wanting a woman who appeared to have no interest in him personally. He stepped out of the shower, dried off, and called a member of his team who handled security checks. It wasn't unusual for him to obtain background checks on people he dealt with.

"How deep do you want us to dig?" his man asked him.

"I want everything," Asher answered abruptly and hung up. Knowledge was power, and he didn't have any problem using it to his advantage. He did hope, however, she didn't give in to him too easily. He met his eyes in the mirror above the bathroom sink. It had been too long since he'd felt this type of anticipation about anything. He saw the light of excitement in his expression and shook his head in amusement.

Emily held the promise of being a tantalizing distraction. He liked that she was passionate about the little museum project she mentioned. If being with her was as good as his cock believed, he'd gift her a piece of property elsewhere, possibly even help her fund her museum. He'd always been a generous lover.

Women didn't turn him down, and Emily would be no different. She was feisty and self-assured; he couldn't wait to see how that translated in the bedroom. His bed to be specific.

Asher dressed in boxer briefs and lounge pants and heated the meal left for him by his housekeeper. He answered emails and read over a few documents in preparation for the next day. When he had no other excuse for delaying any longer, he called his mother. It was only after he'd dialed the number that he checked the time. Shit. It was nearly ten. His mother was probably already asleep, but she'd worry if she saw he'd called, so he stayed on the line.

"It's late, Asher, but it's good to hear your voice. You've been so busy lately. I miss you," she said warmly.

Another mother might have said those same words with the intention of making her child feel guilty. Sophie Barrington never had an ulterior motive. She said it simply because she meant it. His mother was the most loving person he'd ever met. She put the happiness of others above her own. He'd like to admire that trait, but it had prevented her from being able to stop his father's career from imploding. She'd given up, and he would never understand that decision. Still, that didn't stop him from loving her. "Time got away from me, but I didn't want to not call in case it was something important."

"It could have waited, but I did want to speak with you. What did you think of Emily Harris?"

Nothing I could say to my mother, Asher thought. He pushed away the image of her perfectly rounded ass as she'd bent to retrieve something from beneath a chair in Ryan's office. "Why do you ask?"

"Thank you for seeing her today. From the first time I heard it, her story moved me. Your father felt the same way."

"How well do you know her, Mom?"

"Not very, but she spent this afternoon with us, and she is just as sweet and earnest in person as she sounded on the phone. I hated to see her leave. She gave us a painting her mother had made. It's the most incredible thing. When you look at it, you miss the beauty of it. It's all one color. But if you close your eyes and run your hands over it, it's a masterpiece. I cried. Her mother was blind; did she tell you? Remarkable."

Asher's hand tightened on the phone. Although part of him was interested in what his mother knew about Emily, the protective son in him was instantly on high alert. "Mom, don't see that woman again. She is trying to use you to get me to change my mind about buying her property in New Hampshire."

His mother laughed. "I know. She told us. She's not a hard nut to crack. We were her Plan B. How adorable is that? She told us all about how she went to your office and warned you that you couldn't have her land. She also told us what you said. Asher, I raised you better than that. You could have at least promised to look into alternative sites."

Asher paced the length of his living room and growled his displeasure. "This is business, Mom."

"I know, and normally I wouldn't get involved, but blocking a museum for the blind from opening? Really? Asher, I can't stand back and condone that."

"Her museum will open, but not at its present location."

With a pained sigh, Sophie said, "Did you know that her mother gave her that property? It was passed down from her grandfather. When she told me about how she and her mother had created the core artwork for the museum together and what it meant to her, I knew I had to call you. You can't buy her land, Asher. Find another site for your . . . whatever."

"Not possible. My company has invested time and money into that location."

"Asher Dale Barrington, how often do I ask you for anything?"

Fuck. Using his middle name meant his mother was serious. "All I can promise is that I'll contact Ms. Harris and discuss the matter with her again."

"Thank you, Asher. I'm confident that when you hear

more about her project you'll see why you'll have to change your plans this time."

"Consider this handled, Mom. There is no need for you to speak with Ms. Harris again."

"I won't get involved in your business again, Asher, but we did enjoy Emily's company so much we invited her to spend the weekend at our place in Nantucket. She's never been, and there are several resident artists there who could be potential donors for her museum. I'd love to help her acquire some rare pieces. She was so grateful when I mentioned the idea to her. Even your father is excited, and it's good for him to have something to think about besides his health."

Oh, Emily, I underestimated you.

He smiled. He liked the challenge she presented. A rush of anticipation filled him as he considered his next move with her.

Chapter Three

E MILY PLOPPED INTO a seat across from Celeste in a small cafeteria on the first floor of her friend's workplace. Celeste was stylishly dressed in a blouse and skirt that looked both casual and expensive at the same time. Emily was back in jeans and a T-shirt and down to seven acrylic nails. The salads they had both ordered looked mediocre at best, but that didn't matter. It was so good to see Celeste again. Emily looked around the room. "So, do you still love Boston?"

Celeste took a sip of her water before answering. "I love what I do and being here makes sense. It's definitely not Welchton, but that's good in some ways."

Shaking her head, Emily pushed her salad around the bowl. "I can't imagine living anywhere else."

"You've never gone anywhere, so how do you know?"

"That's cold, Celeste. True, but cold," Emily said with a smile.

"Hey, sorry, I didn't mean that the way it sounded. And I'm sorry I rushed you off the phone last night. This latest project is killing me. I hate that I can't drop everything to hang out with you."

Emily shrugged. "You don't have to entertain me, it's just good to see you."

"Same here. Okay, so spill about yesterday. You met with—Sophie and Dale Barrington? Is that what you said their names were?"

Just thinking about it had Emily's stomach churning nervously. How two of the sweetest people she'd ever met had produced someone like Asher was beyond Emily's imagination. She pushed her salad away. "Yes. And they were so nice. I couldn't lie to them."

"Oh, my God, Em. What did you say?"

Despite cheeks that were warm with embarrassment, Emily tried to appear less mortified by her admission. *Okay, so I'm not a sleuth, nor do I want to be.* "I told them everything, including how I'd chosen a hotel near them as part of my Plan B."

"You're lucky they didn't call the police."

"They actually handled it really well. They asked me about a hundred questions then fed me a delicious lunch that will have me dieting for a week. They even invited me to spend the weekend at their beach house on Nantucket Island."

Sitting back in her chair, Celeste shook her head in amazement. "You won them over. I didn't doubt that part. Are you actually going away with them this weekend?"

Emily folded her napkin into a triangle and then folded it again nervously. "Am I crazy if I say yes?"

"The state of your sanity has already been established." Celeste dug through her purse and pulled out a key. "But, if you're going to do this, you might as well stay at my place until you go away with them. I made an extra key for my apartment. Bring your stuff over while I'm at work this afternoon if you want."

Emily rushed out of her seat to hug Celeste. "Do you know how much I love you?"

Celeste hugged her back tightly. "Do you know how much I've missed you?"

Not as much as I've missed you. So much had changed in both of their lives over the past few years. Emily didn't look back. She didn't want to think about all she'd lost. Instead she put all of her energy into making the most of what she had left.

Returning to her seat, Emily pocketed the key and took a deep breath. "This could work, Celeste. I don't want to get too optimistic, but Sophie and Dale were very supportive. They even said they'd talk to their son."

Celeste's eyes rounded. "I wonder how Asher Barrington will feel about that."

Emily raised her chin defiantly. "It doesn't matter as long as this works."

Celeste shook her head slowly. "He's not going to be happy you involved his family."

Emily thought about the ease in which he'd dismissed how important her project was to her. "I wouldn't have had to do it if he'd given me any other option. He didn't care at all, Celeste. Maybe he'll care now." Emily's cell phone rang and some of her confidence wavered when she saw the area code. "It's a local number. Do you think it's him?"

Celeste leaned forward. "Answer it."

Emily braced herself mentally. "Hello?"

"You've been very busy, Ms. Harris. I'm impressed, but you're playing a dangerous game."

"I don't know what you're talking about, Mr. Barrington."

"Call my mother and tell her you're sorry but you won't be able to go to Nantucket this weekend."

Emily took a deep breath. An unintentional, additional opportunity might have just presented itself. "If I do that, will you agree to stop trying to buy my land?"

His bark of laughter was insulting. "Do you honestly think you can blackmail me? Do you have any idea who you're dealing with?"

Emily closed her eyes briefly while she chose the perfect words to express the anger growing within her. "Your sense of entitlement is overshadowed only by your ego, Mr. Barrington. You don't impress me. Nor do you scare me. Your parents are perfectly lovely people. They asked me to go away with them this weekend, and that is exactly what I plan to do."

Asher uttered an expletive, then said, "I admire your tenacity, Ms. Harris. If you involved my family to get my attention, you have it, now stay the hell away from them. A car will pick you up tonight at six. Get in it."

Emily mouthed to her friend. "He's sending a car for me tonight. Is that good or bad?"

Celeste waved a hand in the air frantically. "Not good. You're taking this too far, Em. Go back to New Hampshire, now. Forget about Plan B."

Emily thought about what Celeste had said the day before. Nice wouldn't win against Asher Barrington. *I can make a stand now, or spend the rest of my life wishing I had. You are not getting my lunch money, Mr. Barrington.* In a forceful voice, she said, "Until you change your mind, we have nothing to discuss and therefore no reason to see each other. Goodbye." Emily put the phone on the table beside her salad and looked across at her friend.

"Holy shit," Celeste said. "I don't imagine many people speak to him that way."

Emily picked up her fork and stabbed a tomato. "Maybe more people should. What an arrogant ass."

Celeste reached across the table and took Emily's hand in hers. "As proud as I am of you, Em, I'm worried. You have no idea who you're dealing with. B&H has a reputation for crushing their competition. Asher's not only rich, but he's ruthless in business. I can only imagine what he'd be capable of if someone took him on personally. You may be putting yourself in real danger. Is it worth it?"

Emily put her fork down and straightened her shoulders. "My mother didn't let anyone or anything stop her from doing what people told her was impossible. She could have given up, but she didn't. I couldn't look myself in the mirror if I didn't fight for this."

"Just be careful. Okay, Em?"

"Not this time."

This time I intend to win.

DURING A VIDEOCONFERENCE, Asher was too distracted to listen to the updates from his team in California. Try as he might, he couldn't stop thinking about Emily Harris.

He'd read over her background check repeatedly that morning. There was nothing in it that implied she was anything but a small-town girl who wanted to build a museum so far off the beaten track that not many were likely to visit it. Forcing her to relocate would be doing her a favor. He would have explained that to her over dinner if she'd agreed to meet with him.

Completely ignoring the staff around him, he shook his head in bemusement. Ms. Harris was as brash as she was stubborn. He didn't know another woman, or many men for that matter, who would have spoken to him the way she had. He'd been irritated when he'd discovered Emily was trying to use his parents as leverage against him, but he had to admit watching her try to outmaneuver him was fascinating.

And invigorating.

He excused himself from the meeting and called her hotel. Just as he suspected, she was no longer staying there. He returned to his office and flipped her file open, scanning it until he found what he was looking for. Emily's best friend lived in Boston. He made a quick call and said, "I want a full report on a Celeste Smithfield. Yes, it's urgent. You have fifteen minutes."

He paced his office in anticipation and admitted to himself that this was quickly becoming about more than a parcel of land. He didn't want her around his parents, but it was about more than that, too. He wanted to see her again.

He wanted to know how a seemingly ordinary childhood had created a woman who was so passionate about a project she was willing to risk anything—even his wrath.

Did that kind of passion spill into other areas of her life? Would she be sexually shy and inexperienced or bold and skilled?

How many lovers would she have had?

Asher's hands curled into fists at the idea of Emily with another man. He frowned. He would see her again. Thankfully his phone beeped with the information he needed to make that happen.

Chapter Four

WAKING EARLY THE next day, Emily knew she needed to do something to take her mind off the looming fate of her museum. With Celeste at work, she could either play tourist or slowly chew the last remaining fake nails off her fingers in boredom. In casual slacks and a T-shirt, Emily flopped on the couch with her phone to plan her day. She hadn't visited Boston since Celeste had first moved there, but she remembered loving the variety of museums and restaurants. She'd stayed a week and had left feeling as if she'd only skimmed the surface of what the city had to offer. This time she only had one day and wanted to make the most of it. She made a list of art exhibits she wanted to see and planned her route to get to each.

The buzzer on the wall went off. Emily didn't move at first. If it was Celeste, she had her own key or she'd use her cell phone to call up if she'd somehow forgotten it. Celeste hadn't said she was expecting anyone. *It could be a delivery.* With that in mind, Emily went to the intercom beside the door and pressed it. "Hello? May I help you?"

"It's Asher Barrington. Open the door," Asher ordered.

Emily whipped her hand away from the intercom. She brought a hand to her mouth. *How did he know I'd be here?* She leaned her back against the door. *Okay, stay calm. How doesn't matter. He's here. Maybe he wants to say he's had a change of heart.* She pressed the speaker on the intercom again. She hoped she sounded more confident than she felt. "I told you we have nothing to talk about unless you've changed your mind."

His tone remained infuriatingly authoritative. "I won't discuss this while standing out here."

Let me in. Let me in. Not by the hair on my chinny-chin-chin. She covered her mouth to stifle the nervous laughter her thought had inspired. He wasn't a big bad wolf preying on her. He probably wanted to huff and puff and tell her again how important he was. She pressed the button to open the outer door then rushed to the hall mirror. She hadn't put on makeup, and her hair was tied back in a ponytail. She looked away and told herself it didn't matter. He wasn't attracted to her nor did she want him to be.

She opened the door before he could knock and hoped that was a power move. Celeste's apartment was on the third floor of a building without an elevator. *Would seeing him reveal a slight weakness, like being slightly winded, be too much to ask?* He wasn't. Asher was a man in his prime. She hadn't thought it was possible for him to look better than he had the first time she'd seen him, but khaki pants and a crisp white collared shirt accentuated the golden flecks in his hazel eyes.

She sternly reminded herself she didn't like him and

forced a polite smile. "Come in, Mr. Barrington."

He stopped at the door and leaned down, close enough she could smell the light, masculine cologne he wore. "Asher."

Emily narrowed her eyes and said nothing. She stepped back into the apartment, but he didn't follow. He placed one hand on the doorframe beside his head and challenged her without saying a word. There it was, the cocky confidence she'd witnessed the first time they'd met. Emily was tempted to slam the door in his face, but she wanted to hear what he had to say about the property more than she wanted that one moment of pleasure. "Asher."

He lowered his arm, smiled smoothly, and stepped through the doorway. Emily closed the door firmly behind him. He took a moment to look around, then said, "Nice place."

"I'll tell my friend you think so."

He pinned her with his dangerously sexy eyes. "I've heard good things about your Ms. Smithfield's start-up ad agency. My company is always looking for a fresh voice."

Oh, that's low. Does he really think I'm that easy to manipulate? Emily waved a hand toward the kitchen area. "I'll pass that on to Celeste as well. I would offer you a drink, but I'm sure you're too busy to be staying long."

Asher walked past Emily and sat down on the couch. "I took the day off so we could spend it together."

Emily clasped her hands in front of her and tried not to betray her shock. She walked over to a chair and sat down if only to get off her shaky legs. Asher Barrington took a day off? *And he wants to spend it . . .* "Together?"

He looked as if he were about to smile but didn't. He crossed his feet at his ankles. "I've decided to give you a chance to convince me your project is worth the loss of time and money my company will incur if we walk away from Welchton."

Emily's stomach churned nervously. "How?"

He raised one eyebrow. "That part is up to you."

Emily's eyes flew to his and a crazy thought came to her. For just a moment she thought he might be flirting with her. But that would mean he was attracted to her, and he'd given her no reason to believe that. Emily swallowed hard and stood. "If you're suggesting . . ."

"I'm not, but I'm flattered your mind went there." Asher's voice deepened to a tone that was hot as hell, even though he was essentially mocking her.

With her face flaming with embarrassment, Emily chose anger over the confusing reaction her body was having to the mere suggestion of anything happening between them. "Is this a joke to you? Because it isn't to me."

Asher stood and closed the distance between them. He was so close Emily could see the flecks of green in his eyes. "I've never been more serious. You're an interesting woman, Emily Harris. I find it refreshingly difficult to anticipate your next move. We may be on opposing sides of this issue, but we don't have to be."

The air between them sizzled with a sexual tension that shook Emily. She hadn't allowed herself to see him as more than a threat to her museum. Suddenly he was also a man, a very, very attractive one. *No. Don't let him confuse you.*

He raised a hand to her face and ran a finger lightly along the line of her jaw. Emily gasped and stepped back, breaking the contact instantly. The brief touch sent a shiver of excitement through her; it scared her.

Of all the ways she'd thought she might lose to him, she hadn't considered this one. "The only way we could be on the same side is if you relocate your facility."

"Let's start with our more immediate problem."

Emily refused to retreat again. She raised her chin and asked, "And what is that?"

"There is no way in hell I will allow you to spend the weekend with my parents. Before I leave, you will call them and bow out of going with them tomorrow."

Allow me? Who does he think he is? "Or?" *I can't believe I just asked that.*

"Don't test me on this, Emily."

"I'm not afraid of you." That much was true. Fear was far from what she was feeling in response to his close proximity. Her body was humming with an anticipation she couldn't deny. She reminded herself he was a self-absorbed ass, but her libido didn't care.

"You should be."

Emily searched his face for a hint that he was joking, but he held her eyes with deadly calm. In a voice barely above a whisper she asked, "Do you feel powerful when you threaten women?"

His eyes narrowed. "No one uses my family to manipulate me."

Emily looked away. *Touché.* "I didn't have a choice."

He stepped closer and lowered his face to hers; the heat of his breath warmed her ear. "I'm giving you one now. Take it."

Emily turned to look at him again and wished she hadn't. *Take it?* His husky reply had her head racing with thoughts she didn't want to deal with right then. She should be angry with him. She told herself to focus her energy on figuring out how to get him out of the apartment. All it took, though, was another look into those amazing hazel eyes of his and she was wondering what he would do if she leaned forward and brushed her lips over his. *Stop.* She gave herself an inner shake. *What is wrong with me?* "How do I know I can trust you not to walk out of here as soon as I make that call?"

"You can't, but it's the only way you'll have a chance of getting what you want."

Emily turned away from him and picked up her phone. With distance between them, she was able to think straight again. However it was happening, he was finally willing to at least consider the importance of her project. She had to believe that meant he'd begun to waver on his stance. "Promise me something first."

He neither agreed nor refused her request. He merely held her eyes and waited.

I hope I know what I'm doing. "Promise you'll see my museum before you make your decision."

He looked mildly surprised by her comment but inclined his head in agreement.

With hands she fought to steady, Emily dialed Sophia Barrington's number.

ASHER WATCHED EMILY as she exchanged pleasantries with his mother. His attraction to her wasn't a surprise to him. He'd spent the last few days thinking about her. What he hadn't expected, though, was how intense that attraction was. He wanted her right then, right there. Her resistance to the idea only increased his anticipation of what he considered inevitable.

He would have her.

Emily was a distraction that couldn't have come at a worse time. Even with the well-paid contact he now had in Trundaie, the outcome there was uncertain. He'd hired extra security, put the facility on high alert, and was in the process of hiring informants in the outlying community. His physical presence shouldn't be necessary. His team had initiated similar security protocols in the past. He would videoconference with the site supervisor, ensure they had what they needed, and circle back to them after the weekend. Two days off the grid wouldn't make a difference, but it would give Asher time with Emily.

He couldn't imagine it would take more than a weekend to get her out of his system. He'd spend the weekend enjoying her hot little body, use his time in the area to find a suitable alternate location for her museum, and fly out to Trundaie on Monday. He sent a text to his pilot with instructions to meet him at the airport then a message to his driver to pull up to the front of the apartment building.

Emily ended her call, placed the phone on the arm of the couch, and asked, "Satisfied?"

Not yet. "Are you still packed?"

Her eyes widened. "Why?"

"My driver is waiting downstairs. We fly out in an hour."

Emily shook her head. She looked adorably innocent and confused. "We? I didn't say I'd go anywhere with you."

He almost smiled at how easy the win had been. He had no doubt she'd be in his bed by nightfall. "If you want me to see this museum of yours, I have a limited window of opportunity before I need to leave the country."

She chewed her bottom lip before answering and looked around the room. "I'll need a few minutes to gather my things." She rushed around the apartment, tossed some items into her purse, then disappeared into the bedroom before returning with a small overnight bag.

He put out his hand for the bag. "Ready?"

Emily searched his face for a long moment but held her bag tightly in her hands. "I have to be, right? Just don't forget your promise."

Asher frowned. There was a glimmer of hope in her eyes, and he felt he needed to address it. "Emily, going with you to New Hampshire doesn't mean I'll change my mind."

She smiled at him, the first genuine smile she'd given him, and her beauty rocked him back onto his heels. "I know, but it means you might."

Asher opened the door to the apartment then followed Emily into the hallway and down the stairs. The triumph from a few moments earlier had been replaced by a conflicted feeling he had trouble interpreting.

He wanted her and everything was lining up for that to happen. He was poised for a complete win, but it felt wrong. He watched her hand her luggage off to the driver and frowned again. She was a proud little thing.

He guided her into the back of the sedan and blamed his mood on a lack of sleep the night before. He wasn't the type of man to second-guess a decision or to be overly concerned with how his actions made others feel. For as long as he could remember, all that had mattered was winning. He didn't know what to do with whatever was robbing him from enjoying his victory.

They spent the first few minutes of the ride in strained silence before Asher said, "I've never heard of a museum for the blind. How did you decide to build one?" Although he had extensive knowledge of her background from the file he'd received on her, he wanted to hear it from her.

Emily turned in her seat to face him and love shone in her eyes as she spoke. "My grandfather was an artist. He was never famous, but many people in town had his paintings in their homes. He also worked as a carpenter so he could build my grandmother the house of her dreams. Other homes in the area may rival it for size, but not in beauty nor in heart. His love for her is in the detailed woodwork and the stained-glass windows depicting her favorite birds. He and my grandmother collected artwork from around the world, not because it was worth anything, but simply in celebration of its beauty. She died giving birth to my mother. I can only imagine how he felt when he discovered his only child was blind. My mother's fondest memories were when he would take paintings off the wall and describe them to her as she touched them. It was what inspired her to paint."

The emotion Emily freely displayed made Asher feel unsettled. He didn't know what to do with the feelings they pulled at within him, so he pushed his reaction aside and focused on the facts of her story. He tried but had a hard time imagining how anyone could paint if they couldn't see. His doubt must have shown because Emily leaned toward him and nodded. "I know what you're thinking—a blind painter. Impossible. It's not. My mother's work is proof that when you want something badly enough anything is possible. She pushed the definition of art to a new level. What is a painting? If it were simply an exact replica of what we see then all paintings would look like photos. Computers could create better than the human hand. No, paintings are a physical expression of how the artist feels and sees the world. Some try to define painting as a purely visual representation. My mother argued that people can experience beauty as surely with their fingertips as they can with their eyes. My museum is not the only one of its kind, but it's my tribute to my mother and grandfather. They're both gone now, but what they taught me lives on in me, and it's something I want to share with others."

Asher looked out the window of the vehicle briefly. He'd never had much appreciation for art beyond the investment value of a few choice pieces he'd acquired along the way, but he was moved by the story of Emily's family. That didn't mean he would let her attachment to a particular plot of land sway him into relocating his research facility, but he would look into the cost of moving the house instead of demolishing it.

When he looked back at Emily, she was flushed and clearly embarrassed. "I didn't mean to go on and on like that."

Instinctively he reached out and took her hand. "It's a beautiful story."

Her eyes rounded as she looked down at their linked hands, but she didn't pull away. "I hope so. I plan to make it part of the tour when the museum opens."

The attraction from earlier was back, made exquisitely more intense from the feel of her hand in his. He turned it over, caressing each of her fingers with his thumb, one at a time, slowly. Her breathing deepened, and he knew their closeness was affecting her as much as it was him. He didn't want to talk about what stood between them anymore. He wanted to taste her.

He brought her hand up to his mouth and kissed it gently. She blushed, looked away, then back at him from beneath her lashes. "This is a bad idea." She pulled her hand away from his.

"Is it?" he countered.

She looked so adorably flustered he was tempted to pull her into his arms and kiss her, but he didn't. She needed time, and they had all weekend.

She blinked a few times quickly then said, "I don't like you."

He leaned over and whispered in her ear, "I think you

do."

The car slowed and pulled onto a private airfield, and the conversation was interrupted when the driver opened the back door. Asher offered his hand to Emily to help her out and enjoyed how her mouth rounded as she took in the size of his Boeing 757.

She looked from the aircraft, to him, and back. "Did you write your name on it because it's so small you're afraid to lose it?"

Emily didn't look impressed, and Asher was irritated by her joke. "Size is a statement and one I'm proud of. Why wouldn't I want the Barrington name on it?"

She gave him a bland smile. "I guess."

He ushered her toward it with a hand on her lower back. "You hate it."

She wrinkled her nose and said, "It just seems like a waste of money. Imagine what you could have done with the hundreds of thousands it cost—"

"Seventy-eight million."

Emily stopped and looked up at him. "Are you joking?" She searched his expression and frowned. "That's insane. You didn't pay that much for this."

He shrugged a shoulder and urged her up the steps. "When you see the inside you'll understand why it's worth it."

They stepped inside the gray interior. Emily ran a hand over the glossy walnut trim of a cabinet they passed. She touched the leather of the L-shaped couch that faced a large flat-screen television. "I'm glad you showed me this."

The attendant asked them if they'd like a glass of champagne and a platter of fruit and cheese. Asher answered yes and led Emily to a grouping of plush seats around a walnut table. Once they were settled side by side into their seats, he asked, "Why is that?"

Emily looked around the interior of the plane again before answering. "I won't feel bad at all if you lose a little money when you relocate your facility." She tapped her finger on a strip of gold piping on the material around the window. "I've never seen anything like this before. I mean, what is that, real gold?" He didn't answer her, but she apparently saw the answer in his eyes. "Seriously? This plane wasn't amazing enough without giving it bling?"

Asher wasn't used to being a source of amusement to anyone. "Enough," he said curtly.

Emily's eyes filled with amusement. "Oh my God, did I hurt your feelings? I didn't mean to. I'm sure there are many, many, many people who would love this."

Asher laid a finger across Emily's lips to halt her from saying more. The reprimand was more of a caress . . . and an excuse to touch her tempting mouth. "After takeoff, perhaps you'd like a tour of the other rooms. You might be more impressed with the bedroom and shower."

Emily's cheeks went bright red, and she stammered, "Don't touch me."

A grin tugged at Asher's lips, and he dropped his hand. Emily was a delight. He leaned closer to her and challenged, "Do you always play it safe, Emily?"

The plane picked up speed and took off while Emily

chose her next words. She met his eyes again and demanded, "What are you doing? I thought you wanted to see my museum."

"I do," Asher said. "But that's not why I'm here, and you know it." He took her soft chin within his fingers. "There is something between us that would be a shame not to explore. I cleared my schedule for two days. I know exactly how I want to spend that time, and you can pretend to be shocked, but I've seen the way you look at me."

Emily jerked her chin away from his hand. "You don't have any intention of changing your mind, do you? You're here because you want to have sex with me."

"I could lie and say you're wrong, but I'd rather be honest. Look me in the eye and tell me you haven't thought about what we'd be like together."

Her slap took him completely by surprise. "You bastard."

Adrenaline rushed through Asher as did his anger, but he let neither control him. He rubbed a hand over his cheek. "I didn't expect you to have a temper."

She folded her arms across her chest and glared at him. "I didn't expect you to be a *complete* asshole."

A primal desire to tame her rose within him, and his anger dissolved as images of her writhing in ecstasy beneath him as he thrust deeply into her filled his head. He shifted in his seat as his cock came uncomfortably to a throbbing fullness. No woman had ever tangled him up the way Emily did. If someone had told him a week ago he'd be sitting with a raging hard-on next to a beautiful woman while she called him names, he wouldn't have believed it. What would she say if he told her that her insults only heightened his desire for her? *I like her angry.* The thought made him chuckle.

Emily's eyes narrowed, and her chest heaved with anger. "Don't you dare laugh at me."

He leaned forward and spoke softly into her ear. "I'm laughing at myself. You have no idea how badly I want to fuck you right now." He glanced down at his crotch. Her eyes followed, and he enjoyed how they lingered on him before rising to bravely meet his gaze again. "I've been thinking of little else since you came into my office. I will have you. Maybe not on this flight. Maybe not tonight. But I always get what I want, and I want you, Emily. We both know you want me, too. Fight it all you want; the truth is in your eyes."

The quick inhale of her breath was a tell that pleased him. She kept her arms firmly crossed in front of her. "I would slap you again, but I think you enjoyed it."

"I wouldn't try it a second time, but I do like what it says about you. Inside that good girl is a passionate woman I want to spend the weekend in bed with."

Her cheeks were pink. Her breathing was labored. Asher thought she might turn her head and kiss him, but she didn't. Instead she said, "I wouldn't sleep with you if you were the last man on the planet and fucking you was the only way to insure the future of humanity. Land this plane and get me the hell off it. I don't care if you do take me to court. I'll find a way to beat you there."

"Emily—"

"I don't want to talk to you anymore." She turned her

back on him and looked out the window.

Never in his adult life had anyone turned their back to him. Asher was both offended and excited by the challenge. He was a man who was used to having the upper hand, but Emily had him rethinking his strategy.

He could have forced her to look at him, but he wanted her to want to be with him. The attendant placed food and two flutes of champagne on the table in front of them. Emily kept her face averted. Asher said, "I won't take it as a sign of anything if you eat."

"I don't want anything from you."

Was she afraid? He didn't want that either. He tapped his fingers on his knee. As his hard-on subsided, clear thinking returned. "If my bluntness scared you—"

She turned back to him with eyes that were flashing with anger. "I'm not scared; I'm angry. I knew the first moment I met you that this was who you were, but I guess I'm not a good judge of character because I would have sworn I saw something else in you, too. I thought you actually cared when I told you about my family."

Asher frowned and clarified, "I did care, and I still do, but I don't base business decisions on how I feel about anyone or anything. It muddies the water. I understand your attachment to the property, but even a museum is a business. I can help you find a location that will ensure more traffic."

Emily pressed her lips firmly together and blinked back tears. "Just stop talking." She turned away again.

Asher sat beside her in silence. If she were waiting for an apology, she'd wait a long time. He hadn't done anything wrong. In fact, of the two of them, she was the one who had ventured into a form of blackmail by going to his parents in an attempt to sway his decision. Instead of pouting, she should be grateful he was attracted enough to overlook her Machiavellian methods. Comfortable with how he'd handled the situation, Asher took out his phone and used the quiet time to answer emails.

They'd flown most of the way to New Hampshire without exchanging another word, and Emily had stayed rigidly turned away from him. She hadn't accepted any food or beverage the attendant had offered. He'd expected her to turn and apologize for her mood, but she hadn't. He put a hand on her shoulder and was surprised at the tension he felt there. It was then Asher decided to honor his promise to Emily. He still wanted her in his bed, and didn't doubt the inevitability of that, but he could see how there was one issue that had to be addressed before that happened. "When we land, take me to see this museum of yours."

She shrugged away from his touch. "I think we're beyond pretending you're interested in it."

"Show me the damn building," he growled beside her ear.

Chapter Five

EMILY SUPPRESSED A shiver at the feel of Asher's breath on her ear. She knew giving him the silent treatment on the way over had bordered on childishness, but she was angry. If they had been on the ground instead of thousands of feet in the air, she would have walked away from him hours ago.

She felt duped. *The second he said something that resembled what I wanted to hear, I let myself believe things would work out. Why? Because he's gorgeous? Because when he says he wants me I get a little lightheaded and giddy? That's what he wants and how he'll win.*

I have to be smarter than that.

The plane began to descend and circle a house with a long airstrip. Emily shook her head. She should have known they wouldn't land at a major airport. As soon as the plane landed, she and Asher released their seat belts and stood. Emily took out her phone and turned to Asher. "What's the address of where we are?"

"Why?" he asked, not sounding pleased by her question.

Emily held up her phone with her thumb poised above

the screen. "So I can have a car pick me up. I'm not staying with you a moment longer than I have to."

Asher plucked the phone out of her hand and tucked it into the front pocket of his slacks. "Then it makes sense to not make it too easy for you to leave."

No, you didn't just do that! He was pretty pleased with himself; she could see it in his eyes. "Is that supposed to be funny?"

His gaze was steady and his tone authoritative. "I'll give it back to you once you calm down."

Emily's temper, the one she previously would have denied having, rose within her again. "Calm down? What part of forcing me to stay here will do that? I'm leaving. You can't keep me here against my will. There are laws against kidnapping, or do you feel that you're above those, too?"

He smiled in reaction to her tirade. "I doubt many would consider stopping at my winter vacation home to provide you with refreshments a criminal act." He placed his hand on her lower back and urged her toward the door of the plane.

Emily planted her feet and refused to budge. "As I said earlier, I don't want anything from you. I'm not going inside your house. Give me my phone so I can call for a car."

He turned and bent to issue his challenge. "Or what? What will you do if I don't?"

Emily looked around quickly, noted the flight staff, then put her hands on her hips and said in what she hoped was a low and threatening tone, "I don't want to cause a scene, but I will if I have to."

Asher ran a hand slowly up the back of Emily's neck beneath her hair. There was something both sexual and dominant in the act, and it sent a cascade of confusing sensations through Emily. She wanted to hate it, but a small part of her couldn't deny being turned on by his touch. "Oh, Emily, when will you realize it's not a good idea to threaten me? It usually brings a swift and unpleasant reaction from me." He lowered his voice. "With you, however, it has a different effect. I'll admit I'm enjoying our time together."

She shoved his hand away. "I'm only here because you lied to me. You made me think this trip was about seeing my museum. Otherwise I wouldn't be here."

His eyes narrowed and his nostrils flared. "I don't lie. I don't have to. So let's get one point crystal clear now. Sleeping with me will have no impact on the decision I'll make about your land. I never mix business and pleasure. I am, however, willing to see your museum for the sole reason that the way you've described it piqued my curiosity. I took your phone because if you leave now, you're walking away from your only chance to keep your property. It's a very slim chance, but I'd hate to see you throw it away."

Breathing heavily, Emily snapped, "So you're doing me a favor? Is that how you see this?"

"Yes. You shouldn't let the fact that you'll end the weekend by saying yes to fucking me influence your business decisions." The desire in his eyes removed all doubt that he might be joking.

"I can't be the only woman who has ever hit you."

Asher gave her a lusty look. "You are, and although I prefer pleasure over pain, it definitely put some ideas in my head."

"Then you'll love the kick to the shin I give you if you don't return my phone." Emily held out her hand.

A smile curled one side of his mouth. "You're a violent little thing when you're angry, aren't you?"

Emily took a calming breath and clenched her hands at her side. "Not at all."

He handed her back her phone. "Only for me? I like that." He sounded pleased as he straightened and began to usher her out of the plane again.

Holding the phone tightly, Emily raised her chin and walked down the steps onto the tarmac. She wanted to tell him where to go but didn't. She couldn't risk throwing away her only chance of convincing him to find an alternate site for his facility. She searched his face for a moment. "I'll call Mr. Riggins and have him leave the lights on for us. It gets dark early this time of year."

ASHER SUPPRESSED A grin as Emily shifted even farther away from him as they drove down the winding New Hampshire roads. She was still fighting her attraction to him and probably would until after he made his decision regarding her property. He was okay with that. In fact, he was enjoying the spontaneity of their heated exchanges.

"Tell me about Mr. Riggins," Asher prompted as he wound the car down another mountain road.

Emily turned slightly toward him. "He and his wife are the museum's caretakers. They are helping to get the building ready for the public as well as helping keep an eye on it when I can't. They used to live in the adjacent house until your company bought their home. Now they rent a place one town over."

After meeting Emily, Asher had brought himself fully up to speed on the Welchton project. "They were one of the first to sell. If I remember correctly, they were quite happy with the offer we gave them."

Emily's expression remained carefully calm. "There isn't much work in the area. I don't blame them for taking the money."

Asher watched her expression out of the corner of his eye. "Every single buyout ended with the seller's satisfaction. Some held out for more money, but they all eventually came to an agreement both sides were satisfied with."

Her eyes narrowed. "Some of those homes had been in families for generations. How do you feel about demolishing history?"

Asher turned his eyes back to the road. "It's called progress, Emily. For something new to be built, something old must usually be torn down. Although your sentiments are quaint, they aren't realistic. I offered above market price to your neighbors and they chose money over the history you're suggesting I put value in. What does that tell you?"

Emily let out a harsh breath. "If you offer a loaf of bread to a starving man in exchange for his soul, who is at fault if he takes it? Him for not choosing the harder road, or you for not offering him another alternative?"

Asher knew it wasn't the response she was aiming for,

but he smiled. Although he didn't agree with her view on the situation, it was refreshing to be with an intelligent woman with whom he could debate topics. "Your neighbors were hardly starving. What I did was give them a second chance to have a nest egg for retirement or pay for their children to go to college. My company requires a facility in this area. Would you prefer I offered the money to another town? You claim to care about your community, but do you? It seems to me you're putting your own interests above theirs. They aren't complaining, but they would be if they were still trapped in homes many of them could no longer afford."

"That's what you tell yourself so you can sleep at night?"

Asher shrugged and met Emily's eyes briefly. "It's the way the world works, Emily. You're naïve if you don't see that."

Emily turned to look out the window again. When she turned back she spoke quietly. "I don't agree, and there's nothing heroic or admirable about being jaded."

"I never claimed to be heroic or asked for your admiration," Asher said harshly. Their conversation had moved from interesting to uncomfortably personal.

"Wow. What happened to you? Your parents seem like wonderful, caring people. What made you afraid to be the same?"

Asher slammed on his brakes at a stop sign and gripped the steering wheel. "Fear has no place in my life, but you're right, I'm nothing like my parents."

Emily clasped her hands on her lap. "Isn't it sad that's the first thing we agree on?"

Asher cursed. Their trip wasn't going at all the way he'd planned it. He'd confidently assumed he would be able to convince her to not only sell, but to spend the rest of the weekend celebrating that decision with him. He saw now that he'd been overly optimistic. Emily wasn't what he'd expected at all. She wasn't impressed by his wealth, and she was, by far, the most stubborn woman he'd ever come across. He was used to people retreating from his temper, but Emily wasn't intimidated. In fact, her reprimand still hung in the air between them. Worse, she looked like she felt sorry for him.

Him.

Emily had evaluated him and clearly found him lacking in certain areas. He didn't normally put much thought into what others thought of him, but Emily's opinion mattered. He knew she found him attractive, but with her, he wanted more than that.

As they drove through the area of his proposed facility, they fell into silence. The windows and doors of the homes were boarded up. The lawns were overgrown. The area had the abandoned feel of a ghost town. This was a phase of development Asher had never witnessed in person. He'd read about it in reports. He'd seen photos of areas before the demolition commenced, but he'd never driven through a project site so early on.

He gave himself an internal shake. If he felt anything at all, it was because Emily had planted the idea in him that he should. There was nothing wrong with progress. Change and death were life's only certainties.

Still, when he glanced over and saw Emily's sad expression, he gritted his teeth. He felt compelled to say something, but there wasn't much he could say. They had both made their positions clear.

As soon as he turned onto her street, he was taken aback by the contrast between her property and those around hers. Her building and the park-like lawns that surrounded it looked out of place among the abandoned homes. He parked in the paved lot beside it and walked around the car to open Emily's door, but she had already let herself out.

Her expression warmed with pride as she looked the building over. "Welcome to the Harris Tactile Museum of Art." When she turned to look at him her eyes were bright with tears. "We're finally close to being ready to open."

He wanted to shake her and tell her to look around. She may not want to see how the area had changed, but she was living in denial. There was a reason most museums were in or around cities. The traffic needed to keep a museum open was simply not there. Seeing the place in person reaffirmed his conviction that relocation was her only option.

As they approached the building, he inspected the exterior. He was well traveled and considered himself difficult to impress, but even in the early darkness of the late winter evening, the details in the molding were master carpentry. Just as Emily had said, the two-story home had been built with such attention to detail that it was surely a piece of art in itself.

They walked up the steps together, and Emily unlocked the front door. Asher expected to walk into a home that was in a chaotic state of renovation. Instead, he was surprised by how far along her museum was. The path that led to a payment booth was flanked by a railing, which displayed several Braille signs. Translations of the signs were posted beneath the Braille. Headsets hung on the wall beside the payment booth.

Emily walked ahead of Asher and touched one of the headsets. "This was one of the more expensive renovations, but we're working on an audio tour for the entire museum. It includes music and sounds that go along with the mood of each piece of art. All of our senses are important and even more so when one is limited to fewer of them."

Asher followed Emily through the entrance and down a corridor flanked by large paintings on slanted boards. He stopped at one such station and ran his hand over a self-portrait of Vincent Van Gogh. "Amazing."

Emily stopped beside him and said, "It's a 3-D print donated to my family while my mother was still alive. The original is in a private collection, but I was able to convince the owner that copying the masterpiece for this medium would only increase its value."

Asher looked around and asked, "I'm curious. Why are all the paintings in color?"

Emily stepped away and Asher followed. "There is a wide spectrum of blindness. Many people are visually impaired but can still see color. This allows them to connect what they feel to what they're able to see."

They walked down the main hall together. Off to one side, Asher spotted a room of paintings that were all in one color. He nodded toward it and Emily led the way inside. "My mother painted these. They're an entirely different medium. 3D computer prints take the work of a sighted person and make it accessible for the blind. My mother was blind. Her works were her attempts to give everyone access to how she envisioned the world."

Asher hesitated. Knowing that her mother had created it, and what it represented, gave the experience an emotional depth he wasn't comfortable with.

Emily studied his face for a long moment then said, "Close your eyes."

Asher didn't like that she seemed aware of his level of discomfort. "How many paintings did your mother create?" he asked to distract her.

Emily took one of his hands beneath hers and placed it on one of the paintings. She moved his hand back and forth over the texture of the paint. "Focus on this one. You won't understand what she did unless you let yourself experience it."

Reluctantly, Asher closed his eyes. At first all he could think about was Emily's touch, her nearness, how much just being next to her made him want her. With his eyes closed, he was more aware of how close she stood beside him, the sweet smell of her shampoo.

"What do you feel?" she asked.

Asher held back his first answer and attempted to concentrate on the painting. The painting was layered with many different lines and textures that at first made no sense to him. Slowly, though, an image began to take shape in his mind. Part of the painting was raised in a way that reminded him of sand. It brought back a memory of a lake his parents used to own a home on. The smooth circles of paint reminded him of the rocks he'd skip across the water. There were other details he couldn't describe precisely, but they felt familiar to him. The more he ran his hand across the painting, the more vividly he could recall being on that beach until he could have sworn Emily's mother had painted his memory. Even though he doubted he was correct, he asked, "Is it a sandy beach by a lake?"

Emily's hand tightened on his. "There's a pond behind our property that has a beach. We spent a lot of time there when I was young. My mother loved to hunt for the perfect rocks to throw in. She swore different shapes made different sounds. I could never hear the difference. I preferred flat, smooth rocks I could skip across the water. That memory comes alive for me when I touch that painting, and it's an emotional experience for me."

Asher opened his eyes and tore his hand from the painting. He wasn't ready to admit it had done the same for him. "Interesting."

Emily ran her hand over her mother's work again. "My mother was gifted. She was able to capture the essence of what she'd never experienced visually and do it in a way that connected with everyone who touched her work. People need to feel what she was capable of. Not just visually impaired people. Everyone. She taught me that life is full of challenges, but it's what we do with those challenges that can be truly beautiful."

Asher cleared his throat. He hadn't understood true beauty until that moment. As he looked down at Emily he saw purity and goodness, inside and out. It was a realization that made it difficult for him to reconcile how he felt about her museum with the reality of its fate.

At best the whole building could be relocated. Even though that option was expensive and complicated, seeing it had proven it was an option worth considering.

"Would you like to see my contributions?" Emily asked with a hopeful smile.

There was an innocence in her smile that gave him pause. *She and I couldn't be more different. It takes so little to make her smile, and I'm nearly impossible to please. A woman like that should be with someone less jaded than I am.*

What am I doing here?

He nodded and followed her into an adjacent room that was filled with sculptures of animals and people. Some were recognizable copies of famous sculptures; some were not. Emily walked over to a bust of a woman. "This is my grandmother. It's not my best work because it was one of my earlier ones. My grandmother died giving birth to my mother, but I used old photos to make this. My mother cried for a whole week after I gave this to her. She said they were happy tears. I knew then that I had found what I wanted to do. There are now 3D printers that can create similar sculptures from photos and those will be part of my museum one day, but people can do something computers can't—we can see another person's true essence. I like to think my mother cried because I allowed her to see her mother's soul."

Asher was a man rarely at a loss for words, but when he saw how Emily's eyes had misted over with emotion, he pulled her to his chest and hugged her quietly. *Fuck.*

A moment passed, then two. Asher expected Emily to pull away from him, but she didn't. His heart was beating wildly in his chest, and he wondered if she could hear it. He looked down at her and gave in to the impulse he'd fought all day. He kissed her lightly on the mouth.

It was a kiss unlike any he'd experienced. There was passion in it, but when her lips moved eagerly against his, he felt more. He tasted her sadness, her vulnerability, but also her determination and fire. He brought his hands up to cup her face and kissed her gently. She arched against him, opening her mouth to him, and he knew then she would be more to him than a weekend fling.

He broke off the kiss and rested his chin on top of her head. The only sound in the room was their ragged breathing.

He didn't believe in love.

He wasn't looking for forever.

But Emily Harris would be his, of that he was certain.

Chapter Six

E MILY WAS STILL a little shell-shocked when Asher walked
her down the dark path behind the museum to her
home, which had originally been her grandfather's guest-
house. It was a sliver of the size of the main house, but the
workmanship was just as masterful. If it was a cold night,
Emily didn't notice. Her cheeks were still flushed from the
kiss she'd shared with Asher.

She fumbled with the lock on the front door of her
home. Asher took the key from her and unlocked it. Emily
refused to meet his eyes. *I shouldn't have kissed him. I definite-*
ly shouldn't have enjoyed it.

There was no use lying to herself about how good his kiss
had felt. It had been amazing, the kind a woman waits her
entire life for. *Why does a kiss like that have to come from a*
man like him? There is nowhere good this can go. Okay, yes,
part of me wonders what sex would be like with a man who can
make my body hum for his touch just by looking at me. But how
can I want a man I don't even like? A man who wants to take
my museum from me? My history. I should hate him.

What he wants from me is clear.

It would just be sex.

Uncomplicated, animalistic fucking.

Oh God, why does that sound so good?

Emily thought back to the last boyfriend she'd had who had been incredibly sweet, but had also been shyer than she was when it came to sex. She'd enjoyed the sex. Well, she hadn't disliked it, but it had always left her feeling uncertain about wanting to repeat it. Sadly, he'd appeared to feel the same way.

It wouldn't be like that with Asher Barrington.

He's wrong for me, but I want him so badly I ache for him. Is this what happens when a woman goes a year without sex?

"Are you coming in?" Asher asked in an amused tone. He flipped on the hall light as if he'd been there a hundred times and placed the key on a small table beneath the switch.

Keeping her gaze steady, Emily held the door open behind her. "Thank you for walking me to my door, although there was no need. I hope seeing how close the museum is to completion sways you to at least consider not moving forward with your facility."

Asher walked over, placed his hand over hers, and closed the door behind her, effectively cornering her. "I don't want to talk about the museum anymore today."

Still refusing to look up, Emily said huskily, "You should go."

Asher stayed where he was, looming over her with his head bent so his face was just above hers. "Maybe. Look me in the eye and tell me to."

Emily forced her eyes to meet his, and her breath caught

in her throat at the passion she saw burning there. "I hate everything you represent."

He traced the side of her neck with the back of his fingers. "But you don't hate me."

Emily's body came alive beneath his touch. She shivered and pressed herself back against the door. "No," she whispered and cursed herself for the admission.

"Good," he said and lowered his mouth to graze the side of her face with kisses. "I want you. Tonight. Take me to your bed." He pushed her hair over her shoulder and began to kiss the curve of her neck. "Say yes, Emily."

Emily kept her hands clenched at her sides, but she couldn't stop herself from closing her eyes as desire rocked through her. Renovating the museum had been a lonely project, but she hadn't realized how lonely until just then. Her life had once been full of affection and physical displays of love. It had been a long time since she'd been held, and Asher's touch moved her on many levels. Her body was quivering with hunger for him; her soul craved the intimacy he offered. He had barely done more than kiss her neck and she was wet and ready to rip her clothing off right there in the hall. *Be strong.* "You should go."

He stopped and raised his head. "You know it would be good between us."

"Just because something feels good doesn't make it right."

He ran his hands up and down her arms. "It doesn't make it wrong, either."

Emily tried to take a step back but his hands closed on

her arms. "You think you have all the answers, but you don't. Look at me. I'm not whoever you're confusing me with. I'm not going to sleep with you just because you look at me with those stunning eyes of yours."

He smiled. "You like my eyes."

She glared at him. "I'm an artist. I appreciate beauty wherever I find it."

"What else do you like?" he asked, clearly amused.

Emily pressed her lips together then said, "I can't see anything beyond your swollen ego."

He laughed out loud and pulled her against him. His cock pressed proudly against her. "It's not my ego that's swollen."

Desire shot through Emily, but she fought the urge to bring her hands up to touch his cock. She melted against him, and tried to sound angry as she fought for control. "Get your hands off me."

He released her. "So scared. Where is the brave woman who came to Boston to threaten me? That woman knew what she wanted and wasn't afraid to go after it."

"I'm not afraid."

He shook his head. "Aren't you? Why else would you say no to something we both know you want?"

Emily folded her hands across her stomach. "I'm not a casual sex kind of person, that's all. I won't sleep with someone I don't love."

His eyes narrowed. "How many times have you been in love?"

"That's none of your business."

A smile twisted his lips. "My bet is never."

"I'm not a virgin, if that's what you're implying."

"I'm not, but you also weren't in love with those men. I know it. You know it. Dress it up however you want, but at the end of the day, it's all the same. Do you want me to tell you I love you? Is that how they got into your bed? I won't. I don't lie. I want to fuck you, Emily. That's it. I want to taste every inch of you until you're wet and ready for me. Then I want to pound into you while you call out my name, begging me to fuck you harder. That's what I want. What about you?"

"What happens tomorrow?" She forced herself to ask the question, but she was quickly losing interest for the answer.

Asher made a sound in her ear that was half growl half purr. "I doubt we'll get out of bed tomorrow. I intend to savor every inch of you." He unsnapped the front of her slacks and slid a hand beneath her panties. "You're already wet, Emily." He dipped a finger between her lower lips and sought her clit. Pleasure rocked through her when he began to lightly circle it with his middle finger. "Don't fight it. Give yourself to me."

There were many, many, many reasons why Emily should have said no, but she brought her hands up to his face and pulled his mouth to hers. One night. Okay, and also the next day. She'd spent her life doing the right thing. She was not done fighting for what she believed in, but didn't she deserve a brief reprieve?

For just one night she didn't want to be the devoted daughter and granddaughter who still mourned the loss of the two people she'd loved most in the world. She didn't want to think about how close she was to losing her dream or how the man who was delighting her might play a part in that loss as well. She kissed him and released her pent-up yearning and need.

He broke off their kiss long enough to ask her where the bedroom was. She could have used that moment to regain her sanity and ask him to leave, but she didn't. She pointed to her open bedroom door and met his next kiss halfway. The light reflecting off the snow outside illuminated the house enough for Asher to be able to find her bed.

He placed her on her feet beside it and turned on a lamp. He stripped off his clothing and stood in front of her with his erection proudly displayed. Emily took a moment to appreciate the perfection of him. Like the rest of him, his cock was large, and she couldn't resist reaching out and encircling it with her hand. Wide. Hard. She licked her lips and brought her gaze back to his.

While looking into her eyes, he effortlessly removed her shirt and bra. His hands were gentle but firm, and he caressed each area as he exposed it until she was on fire for him. Emily wasn't normally aggressive in the bedroom, but she ran her hands over all of him urgently and teased her breasts across his chest. Every place they connected made her want him more.

He took his time in a tender way that his earlier boldness hadn't implied. They rolled onto the bed together. He used his body to cushion her fall then rolled on top of her. He positioned himself between her legs and continued to kiss her. His mouth was everywhere, leaving a trail of fire and need in its wake. He kissed his way down between her breasts, down her stomach, and met her eyes briefly before parting her slit and bringing his mouth down on her sex.

When his tongue flicked expertly back and forth across her clit, Emily gripped his shoulders tightly and came to the realization that oral sex came in many different flavors. If asked about it before Asher, Emily would have said it was something she enjoyed. It was a pleasant form of foreplay.

What Asher was doing to her was overloading her senses. It was so intense she almost pulled away at first and then heat rushed through her, making her a slave to his touch. He drove a finger inside her, caressed another against her anus, and kept flicking that tongue. She dug her hands into his hair and held him there, desperate for the sensation to continue.

And it did. Asher pushed her past what she thought she was capable of feeling and continued his intimate assault, even as she cried out and came against his mouth. His touch slowed and turned gentle again as she floated back to earth after her orgasm.

Still in a closed-eyes and sated daze, she heard the opening tear of a condom wrapper. Her sex clenched in anticipation of the pleasure she knew he'd bring. He kissed her deeply, and the taste of her own juices drove her wild in a way she hadn't known possible. He kissed her breasts, but this time his passion gave his mouth a roughness. Emily arched upward, eagerly offering herself to him.

She was running her hands up and down his chest when

he raised one of her legs to his shoulder and thrust himself deeply into her. She almost came again from the power of it. There was no time to recover, no time to think. He took her with a force that brought out unexpected wildness in her. She grasped at his back, opened herself even wider for him, and begged him not to stop. When she came the second time, he joined her with one final deep thrust and claimed her cry of climax with a kiss. "Mine," he growled.

He stayed within her, holding his weight off her with his elbows, and kissed her forehead. The word *mine* reverberated around her mind.

Part of her wanted to protest. Having sex with him may have changed what she'd thought she knew about her own sexuality, but it hadn't changed how she felt about him. When she met his eyes there was a possessiveness she hadn't seen before. Excitement and fear shot through Emily. He'd said he would have her, and she'd given herself to him.

Now he wanted to own her.

For now.

She'd let the big bad wolf in the door, into her bed, and the look in his eyes told her he intended to take full advantage of both. A man like him could swallow her up, destroy everything she'd worked for, and leave her with nothing. Her head knew the only sane thing to do would be to ask him to leave and make the battle between them once again a professional one. She searched his face for a long moment. She'd survived the loss of her grandfather and then her mother. The goal of finishing her mother's dream had given her strength. He could take all that from her. "Don't hurt me, Asher." She hadn't realized she'd said the words aloud until he frowned and rolled off her.

He cleaned himself off and pulled her back into his arms. His voice was gruff when he said, "If I was too rough—"

She raised a hand to his cheek and closed her eyes briefly. "You weren't. I wasn't referring to that."

He took her hand in his and kissed it then tucked her more tightly against his side. He let out a long breath. "I know what you want me to say, Emily, but you're wrong to cling to this place. You may not want to see it, but even if I don't buy your land, everything that would have made your museum a success here is already gone. I can't change that, but I can help you recreate it in Boston or in New York. Name the city, and I'll start crunching numbers."

Emily fisted a hand against his chest. "You're wrong. I will open my museum here. And it will be everything I know it can be."

"You're fighting a battle that's already lost."

Emily pushed away from him, but he held her there until she stopped struggling. A myriad of confusing emotions were rushing through Emily, but she focused on the one she understood. "If you take my land from me, I will hate you forever. Nothing else will matter. It's something I could never forgive you for."

"Is that a threat?" he asked.

She shook her head and spoke from her heart. "No, it's the truth."

ASHER'S ANSWER WAS to kiss her deeply. He wouldn't make

false promises to her, but he did care about her. They made love again, slowly this time. Asher took time to appreciate every curve on the woman he was drawn to in a way he'd never been to anyone. There was a goodness in her that made him want to see her succeed. Asher held Emily until she fell asleep, then slid out of bed, stepped into his pants, and put the distance of a room between them. He paced her living room and reflected on the last few weeks. Before Emily, his greatest concern had been his expansion into Asia and the volatile government of Trundaie, and he had relished the challenge. How had he become a man who was second-guessing how he'd chosen to live his life? Emily was passionate about art, her museum, and making both accessible to all. In the end, the world would be a better place because she was in it.

He doubted the same could be said about him.

He ran through possible scenarios of how Emily's dream could happen in Welchton and each one was more ludicrous than the last. Reselling the homes he'd purchased would get him some of his investment back, but it wouldn't help Emily. Many of the homes had been vacant for long enough to have dramatically reduced in value. The families who had left wouldn't return. He couldn't believe he was even considering relocating his facility away from Welchton.

What was it about Emily that had him all turned around? He'd never let anyone influence a business decision. What did it say about how he felt about her that he wanted to wake her and tell her he would do anything to keep her with him?

Anything to keep her with me? What the hell am I thinking? I'm heading off to Trundaie and back to my life. The last thing I need is to let a woman distract me.

It wasn't just any woman, though. It was Emily. Just the thought of her lying in her bed in the other room made his heart beat loudly in his chest. Trusting his instincts had always guided him well, and everything in Asher was certain of one thing—Emily was his. He hadn't changed his mind about some things. This wasn't forever, but it also no longer had a shelf life of only a weekend. When it ended, which he was certain it would, he would be generous to her, kinder than he'd taken the time to be to anyone. He had a feeling that being with her would leave him changed, and the idea was becoming more appealing to him.

As in business, Asher found power as soon as he chose his path. People wasted time and opportunities when indecisive. Asher had always preferred to set his course, plow through the obstacles, and leave the waffling to those too afraid to fight for what they wanted.

He called his assistant and told him to contact the team and tell them the project was on hold. He'd have his facility and Emily would have her museum. He'd sort out the details once he returned to his office.

"How do you want to handle Blue Ridge Construction? They're waiting for us to return the contract they sent over. They'd hoped to started demolition next month. It's a major project for them," Ryan said.

Asher walked over to the window and took in the outline of Emily's museum against the white of the snow. "Email our contact and tell them we're not moving forward with the facility at this time. There has been a complication."

"Is it the Harris woman? If so, Hearne is back from Germany. He's the best when it comes to resolving complications."

Asher ran a hand through his hair impatiently. As his company had expanded he'd relinquished more and more of the day-to-day decisions to key people he trusted within his company. Ryan was one of those people. His title was personal assistant, but he was paid generously because he could make things happen and with more efficiency than many vice presidents Asher knew in other companies. Still, it was disconcerting to realize Ryan knew more about this Hearne man than he did. "When I get back to the office have a full report on Hearne ready for me."

"I don't ask how he does it, and he doesn't tell me. But if you want Ms. Harris to change her mind, send Hearne to Welchton."

"Keep Hearne out of Welchton and get me that report," Asher said. He hung up the phone and rubbed a hand over his face. Work was usually his priority, but what he wanted right then had nothing to do with his business goals. He wanted a few more days of feeling how he did when Emily smiled at him.

If any of his brothers had spoken about a woman that way, he would have laughed at them. Unfortunately, there was nothing funny about how he felt about Emily. She was an addiction he wanted to lose himself in.

Despite the sex they'd had, he knew Emily was close to

pulling away from him. She was angry about things that had been put into motion before he'd met her. He wasn't the type to apologize, but he'd discovered the pleasure that could be found in not fighting with her, and he wanted to find a way to appease her.

He conceded his lack of expertise when it came to the workings of the female mind and called his sister. "Kenzi, I need your opinion on something."

"Asher? Wait, can you repeat that? Did you just ask for my opinion?"

Asher smiled. Of all his siblings, he got along with his sister the best. Regardless of her sarcasm, he knew she was happy to hear from him. "Do you want to know why I called or not?"

"Is it an apology because you forgot my birthday last week?"

"Did I? Shit. Ryan usually sends—"

"Ryan?" Kenzi asked. "We talked about this last year. I don't want something your assistant picks out for me."

"Which is why you got nothing this year."

Kenzi laughed. "You are so lucky I love you."

"I'll buy you something when I get back to Boston. Now back to my question. You're a woman."

"If that's your question, I'm worried."

"Forget it. I'm not fucking doing this—"

Asher was about to hang up on his sister when she quickly said, "No, wait. Sorry. Ask me anything."

Asher's need for the information outweighed his desire to avoid the conversation. There was a chance his sister might have an idea he hadn't considered. "If you were a woman who didn't care about money, and I had *possibly* done something to offend you, what would smooth that over?"

This time Kenzi didn't answer with a joke. "Without knowing who you're talking about, I can't give specific ideas, but I'd suggest you show her that you care about something she cares about. Take her someplace you know she'd love or to see something you know she's always wanted to see. Does that help?"

Asher started searching on his phone even as he continued to talk to his sister. "Maybe."

"Is there any chance this is the same woman Mom told me about? The one with the museum in New Hampshire?"

Asher decided to neither confirm nor deny the accuracy of his sister's guess. His silence, however, proved to be enough of an answer for her.

"Oh my God, it is, isn't it? Mom will be thrilled. She's convinced this is the woman you should marry. I can't wait to meet her."

"Good night, Kenzi."

"Wait. If this is about Emily Harris, I have the perfect place for you to take her. After Mom told me about Emily's museum, I did an online search to find out more. Do you know that even the Louvre has a tactile exhibit for the visually impaired? If you want to say you're sorry, Asher, take her to Paris. No one can stay angry in the city of love."

Chapter Seven

EMILY WAS NAKED and curled up against Asher, still in a rosy, sated daze after what could only be described as a marathon of the best sex in her life, when he asked her a question she didn't believe she'd heard correctly. "Hmm?"

"Do you have a passport?" he asked again, running a hand lazily up and down her spine.

"Why do you want to know?" Emily asked, then winced at the guarded tone she'd used. It was a dose of reality into what was otherwise a heavenly morning. She'd shared her body with him, but she didn't trust him yet, and what did that say about the quality of her decision?

He didn't appear put-off by her tone. He gave her bare ass a light smack. "I'm taking you somewhere and need to know if the trip will involve paying someone to expedite a passport for you."

Emily pushed herself up onto one elbow. "I can't go anywhere right now. There are only about a million loose ends to tie up before the museum is ready. Going down to Boston already set me behind on my schedule."

"What if I told you I'm putting my project in Welchton

on hold?"

There was something icky about that correlation between what was happening between them and that decision. She pulled the bed sheet over her. "I'd say if it's contingent on me continuing to sleep with you, don't. I'd rather battle it out with you in court than buy the win with sex."

He gave her an odd look. "I really never know what you'll say." His expression turned wolfish as he said, "This has nothing to do with your museum. It's about being nowhere done with you yet."

His words sent desire licking through her, but it didn't dislodge her uncertainty. "Then why put your project on hold?"

His kissed her shoulder. "You convinced me that your museum and its location is worth at least considering leaving as it is. When I return to Boston I'll crunch numbers, estimate the projected loss, brainstorm with my team on how we could recoup the money, and see if I can come up with a plan that makes sense."

Emily let out a shaky breath. "So you're still making up your mind."

Asher tucked a curl behind her ear. "I won't move forward with any decision that adversely impacts my company, but if we can absorb the loss, possibly as a tax write-off, I see no reason why I couldn't relocate my facility."

His words circled around in her head, sounding worse each time she replayed them. She tucked the sheet tighter around her and told herself to be smart about how she extricated herself from the situation. He was saying she had a chance of getting what she'd been fighting for. Losing that just because her pride was dented would give her a moment of satisfaction then a whole lot of regret. She skirted toward the edge of the bed, hoping that putting distance between them would give her the clarity of thought needed to sort out the mess she'd gotten herself into.

He sat up. "So, the question remains—do you have a passport?"

Emily stood and picked up her shirt from beside the bed, then stepped into her underwear. She sounded angrier than she'd meant to when she said, "I do, but I really can't go anywhere right now."

Gloriously naked, he stood and blocked her retreat. "What's wrong?"

"Nothing."

He took her chin in his hand and tilted her face up so she was forced to meet his eyes. "I don't lie to you. Don't lie to me."

All caution fell to the side and Emily pushed his hand away as her temper and voice rose. "Maybe. Possibly. There is a chance that you might save something that means everything to me, but only if it's convenient for you? Do you hear yourself? I won't pretend that I didn't enjoy last night and this morning, but you make me angrier than anyone I've ever met."

Asher's lips pressed together and he frowned. "I can't simply end a project that is this far along just because we—"

Emily wagged an angry finger at him. "Don't say it. Don't you dare say it." She hitched the sheet higher around herself and said, "You should go now. I know I should care how this affects your decision, but right this second, I don't. I want you to get out of my house and stay the hell away from me."

Asher's frown deepened. "I put my project on hold. For you."

Emily waved her hands angrily in the air, not caring that the sheet fell to her feet. "On hold? You don't get it." She rubbed her forehead roughly. "Or maybe I don't. Maybe you are so used to sleeping with people you don't give a shit about that; this is normal for you. It's not normal for me. I made a huge, huge mistake last night and this conversation is just bringing that truth home once again."

Asher looked at her for a long moment then said, "I'll shower first or you can join me. Pack for weather slightly warmer than here. If we leave within the hour we can be in the air by noon."

The whole conversation felt unreal. "I'm not going anywhere with you."

Asher closed the distance between them and pulled her flush against him. One glance at his cock revealed that their conversation had excited him rather than convinced him to leave. "I don't know what we have or if it can possibly last, but I know we won't figure it out here. Your cute little ass can come with me willingly, or I'll pick you up and carry you onto my plane, but I'm taking you to Paris."

Emily's mouth dropped open. "Paris?" It was the last place she'd expected him to want to take her. "Why would we go there?"

His expression softened. "The Louvre has a tactile exhibit similar to your museum. It was going to be a surprise."

Sure she'd heard him wrong, she shook her head to clear it and asked, "You want to take me to Paris to see an exhibit for the visually impaired?"

With his hands on her hips, he held her against him, his cock grazing her inner thighs. "It sounded like something you would enjoy."

She brought a hand to her mouth and her eyes filled with tears. She didn't know if she loved him or hated him in that moment because both emotions were raging wildly within her. She was turned on, pissed off, and touched by his thoughtfulness all at once. "I don't know what to say."

He lifted her up into his arms and carried her toward the bathroom. He gave her a lusty grin and said, "Let's continue this conversation after we shower."

She squirmed in his arms, but it was only a token gesture of protest. Her body and her mind were racing. *Paris with Asher?* Further thought soon became impossible as Asher joined her beneath the hot spray of the shower and began to tenderly wash her. Despite her confusion, there was no denying how young and sexy Asher made her feel. Because of that confusion she'd slept with him the night before and was now seriously considering going away with him.

After so much time alone, being with someone felt good. Being with Asher felt better than anything she'd experienced. That kind of good was terrifying because she knew all too well how quickly things could end.

Later, after they were both dressed and Asher was packing her luggage into the trunk of his car, Emily excused herself to go back into her house. She said she'd forgotten something, but what she actually sought was a minute or two of privacy.

She stepped into her bedroom, closed the door behind her, and quickly called her best friend. "Celeste?"

"Hey, how is New Hampshire? Did it work out that Asher went with you?"

Knowing she was short on time, Emily blurted, "I slept with him, now we're flying off to Paris because he wants to show me a museum there. Have I lost my mind?"

Celeste made a surprised sound. "Wait a second. Back this story up. The last time you texted me you said you were taking him up to Welchton to show him your museum. He was still undecided about what he was going to do. Does this mean he isn't buying your land? Your museum is safe?"

Emily sat on the edge of her bed and buried her face in one hand. "He doesn't know what he's going to do."

"Oh, Em. What are you doing?" Celeste asked, concern thick in her tone.

"I was hoping you could tell me. I want to hate him, but I can't. He says things that make me angry, and he's brutally honest about how important his company is to him. According to him, it's all that matters. We couldn't be more different. But then there are moments when we connect. I showed him my mother's work and he got it. Not everyone does. And then there's the sex. Celeste, I didn't know it could be this good. At first I thought it had been so long since I've been with someone and that's all it was, but this is different. I can't explain it, but it is. He asked me to go to Paris, and I want to. I want to be young and free for just a couple days, and then I'll come back and finish my museum. I can't even believe I said that. See why I need you? Have you ever heard me talk like that? You've known me forever; what is wrong with me?"

Celeste sighed, and she took a moment to answer. "Nothing, Em. Listen, you've been through a rough couple of years. You lost your grandfather and then your mother. That's huge. And you didn't give yourself time to grieve. You threw yourself into finishing your mother's project, and I know you said it made you happy, but you didn't put aside any time for yourself. You haven't dated anyone since your mother died. You're lonely, Em. And Asher Barrington, God, I don't know a woman who would say no to Paris with him. There is nothing wrong with you. In fact, I think you need this."

"What happened to thinking he was dangerous?"

"I'm more afraid of what will happen if you don't go. I'm going to say something that may upset you, but you need to hear it. Lately, I've been worried about you. You used to care about a lot of things, but over the past few years your world has become smaller and smaller until you can't see anything past your grandfather's house and this project. It's not healthy."

Hurt, Emily snapped, "I thought you understood why the museum is important."

"I do, but I also worry about what will happen if it doesn't work out the way you imagine it will."

"You don't think I can do this?"

"Stop. I'm on your side. You called me for my opinion, and I'm giving it to you. Go to Paris with Asher and forget about everything back here for a few days. I'm not saying you should trust him, but if being with him helps you find the Emily Harris I know, then you should go. You've always been a crazy artist, amazingly creative and so full of life. I remember wishing I could be as passionate about something as you were about your sculptures. I know the museum is important to you, but it's not all you are. It's okay to do things simply because you enjoy them. You're going to finish what you and your mother started, Em. I know you will. But you need a life, too."

If the advice had come from anyone else, Emily could have dismissed it and told herself they didn't know her. She and Celeste had been as close as sisters since early childhood. Celeste spoke out of love, and her concerns helped Emily understand what she had been feeling. "I'll text you updates."

Celeste chuckled. "Every day or I'll hunt you down over there." She paused a moment, then asked, "Are we good?"

Emily nodded even though her friend couldn't see it. "We're good." Emily smiled. "Hey, Celeste, guess what?"

"What?"

Giving in to the playfulness of the decision, Emily whispered in excitement, "I'm going to Paris."

LEANING AGAINST THE side of the car waiting for Emily, Asher checked his messages. He answered several emails regarding a variety of projects. When he read an email from one of his men in Trundaie he decided to add a work component to his trip to Europe. He'd spend some time with Emily in Paris, then let her explore the city a bit on her own while he flew over to Trundaie, and then fly back with her when he'd completed his business. Things were working out perfectly.

His phone rang. Surprisingly, it was his brother, Ian. There weren't many subjects on which he and Ian saw eye to eye, so they didn't speak often. Usually Ian was the harbinger of family news. Hopefully it wouldn't interfere with the closest thing to a vacation Asher had taken in a decade. "Ian."

"Asher, Andrew called this morning. He'll be in Boston near the end of April on a one-week leave. Mom wants everyone to stay over while he's there."

"I'm flying over to Europe today. I have a lot going on right now. I'll be there if I can be."

"This is important. You know how she gets around this time of year."

Asher wasn't willing to reopen the topic of why. More harshly than intended, he growled, "I'll be there if I can."

"Make it happen," Ian said in a tone that reminded Asher of their father, which wasn't surprising since Ian was Dale Barrington's clone. Hopefully his political career fared better. "Hey, Mom told me to suggest you bring your girlfriend with you. I didn't realize you had just one or that any of them would be the type Mom would like, but she's talked about this one so much I am curious about her. Emily something. She sounds nice. What the hell is she doing with you?"

Asher glanced hopefully at the door of Emily's house. Any reason for ending the call then would have been welcome. "Do me a favor and explain to Mom that she's looking for fire where there isn't even smoke." It was a lie, but a necessary one. The less his family knew about Emily the better, especially if wedding bells were already ringing in his mother's head. He never introduced the women he dated to his family, and he wasn't about to start with Emily. He couldn't explain how he felt about Emily to himself; he wasn't about to try with anyone else.

"I'm not explaining anything. If dreaming about you getting married keeps her mind off the past, I'll help her pick names for your fucking kids."

"Thanks," Asher said sarcastically. He understood Ian's stance, but he wasn't about to encourage it. Most of the time their mother was upbeat and active. During April of every year for the last twenty-seven years, though, she'd teetered on depression. As young children, he and his siblings had been afraid of the depth of her grief. As adults they understood her pain was from a loss that had an anniversary. "Tell her I'll be there."

"Should I say you're bringing anyone with you?"

"No, because I'm not," Asher said and hung up on his brother as soon as he saw Emily exit the door of her home. She shot him a tentative smile he found adorable, considering how intimately they knew each other. He pushed off the side of the car and met her halfway up her path. "Did you find what you were looking for?"

She searched his face before answering. "Yes and no."

She didn't volunteer more, and he didn't push her to explain. He walked her back to the car and helped her in before walking around to his side. Once they were on a main road and headed toward his home, he took her hand in his and laid it on his thigh. It was a simple touch but one that elicited a strong reaction in him. She belonged with him, to him. He wasn't normally a possessive man, but that was the only way he could describe how he felt around her. Although he'd read her background check, it only skimmed the surface of what he wanted to know. "You've never mentioned family beyond your mother and grandfather."

Emily's hand clenched on his thigh, then relaxed. "I don't have any."

"What about your father?" Asher asked. He didn't like to think of her without a network of family. Although his family drove him crazy most of the time, they would be there for him if he needed them.

Emily pushed a wayward curl back into her ponytail. "My mother met him during the one year she went to college. She said they loved each other very much but his family didn't approve of her. They saw her as a burden. They couldn't have known her at all because she wasn't—not one day of her life."

The idea of any man tossing Emily and her mother aside filled Asher with an anger that had no outlet, so he kept it where he kept the rest of his emotions, locked deep inside. "Did you ever meet him?"

Emily's hand shook slightly below his. "I thought about it once. I have his name, and I considered tracking him down, but I decided not to. If he loved my mother at all, he did a poor job of it. Why would I think he'd make a good father?"

The touch of sadness in her voice moved him in a way not much else did. He was a man of action who allowed himself very little time for deep reflection. In some ways, he and his brother Andrew were more similar than either liked to admit. When the then eighteen-year-old Andrew had announced he had joined the Marines, not many people in their circle had understood why he would choose to risk his life when he could have safely lived off his trust fund. Asher had understood. There had been a feeling of quiet desperation in their home when they were young that none of them acknowledged, but each of them overcame in their own way. Asher and Andrew had each gone to battle: Asher in the business world and Andrew on actual battlefields. Normally discussing family issues brought Asher back to a time when he'd had less control over his life, and therefore, he avoided those topics with his friends and most definitely with his female companions.

It was different with Emily. He felt her sadness as if it were his own, and it confused him. It took listening to her talk about her museum and her family for him to realize how little he cared about anything outside of work. He loved his family, but he didn't go out of his way to see them. He was too busy. "Your father might not know you exist."

Emily's expression hardened. "Then shame on him. If he

never cared enough to look in on my mother to make sure she was okay after he left her, then he doesn't deserve to know about me."

It was a harder stance than he would have imagined Emily taking on any topic, especially one of family. The way she passed judgment on her father left him feeling unsettled. Emily had strong ideas when it came to what was important to her and often her beliefs were in direct opposition with how he lived his life. "I would have thought you'd advocate forgiveness for all."

Emily gave him an odd look. "Then I guess you don't know me very well."

He laced his fingers with hers. They were quiet for a moment and her comment hung in the air. He was used to women trying to impress or flirt outrageously with him. More often than not they talked about fashion or the latest gossip. Emily wasn't like that. She was . . . real, and it took some getting used to.

Emily was the first to break the silence. "What about you? You're the oldest of six? It's hard to imagine you with your family."

He raised an eyebrow as he asked, "Why is that?"

Emily waved her free hand in the air. "I've probably watched too much television. When I imagine a big family, I picture everyone sitting around an enormous table and teasing each other mercilessly." She looked him over. "Laughing."

"You don't think I'm funny?" he asked with a straight face.

Emily met his eyes and said, "Tell me a joke and I'll let you know."

That was a part of Emily he enjoyed. She pushed him beyond his norm. Asher wasn't known for his humor, but he wasn't one to back down from a challenge either. "What makes every snowman smile?"

Emily shook her head. "I don't know."

"Snowblowers."

Emily's expression remained as serious as his then she burst out laughing. "That is the lamest joke I've ever heard."

Asher remembered thinking the same thing when Andrew had told it to him. "One of my brothers considers himself a connoisseur of one-liners, and his time in the Marines has only added to his repertoire."

"Are you close to your brothers?"

"Not very," Asher said, and in that moment the admission wasn't one he was proud of. From the outside his family looked as close to perfect as any family could. His parents were still happily married. Each of his siblings had done well in their chosen careers. They hardly fought. They weren't a big enough part of each other's lives to have anything to argue about. It was his parents who pulled them back together again and again. Without his parents, Asher was reasonably certain interactions with his brothers and sisters would be nearly non-existent.

"Tell me about them," Emily requested as if she could sense the conflict within him.

If anyone else had asked, Asher would have changed the subject, but he didn't. The rest of the drive to the plane flew by as he fielded questions from Emily about his family. He usually kept his private life just that—private, but Emily's interest was sincere, and he found himself sharing stories with her unlike he'd ever done with others.

He and Emily were settled into their seats on the plane when she started tapping the tips of her fingers and said, "Don't help me. Let's see if I can do this. It's you, then Grant, Ian, Andrew, Lance, and Kenzi. Am I right?"

"You've got it."

"Thank God your mother finally had that girl or you might have been one of a dozen."

Asher frowned. "Why do you say that?"

Emily shrugged. "Five boys then a girl. I'm just guessing, but it makes sense that she'd stop there."

"That wasn't why my parents didn't have more children." As soon as he'd said it, he regretted it. He knew why his mother fought depression every year and why his family was quietly dysfunctional, but he preferred not to think about it. There was no avoiding returning to Boston, though, for the week his mother was planning. A week of collectively pretending they didn't know why they were gathered. *Shit.*

Sensing his mood change, Emily laid a hand on his arm. He expected her to ask the question he had no intention of answering, but she didn't. She simply gave him a long steady look, then asked, "What do you call two jalapeños having sex?"

He shrugged. Talking about his family had soured his mood. If he were alone he would have shaken it off by diving into work. For just a moment he felt trapped.

With an absolutely serious expression, Emily finished the joke. "Fucking hot."

A chuckle started deep in Asher's chest. *How does she know what I need when we barely know each other?* He didn't understand how he and Emily connected as they did, but they did. His mood lifted. He unbuckled her seatbelt and pulled her into his lap. "That's worse than mine."

Emily wrapped her arms around his neck. "In your opinion."

He nuzzled her neck. This is what he'd sought—the sweet escape of her touch. When he was with her, everything else faded in importance and he was just a man spending time with his woman. "Do you always have to have the last word?"

Emily ran her hand through the back of his hair and with an impish smile on her face replied, "Yes. What are you going to do about it?"

That's all it took for Asher's cock to leap to full attention. He stood and carried Emily into the plane's bedroom and tossed her onto the bed. "I know one way to keep you quiet."

Emily rolled onto her stomach and purred playfully, "Only one? Now that's disappointing."

Asher laughed. He stripped off his shirt and crawled onto the bed beside her.

Challenge accepted.

Chapter Eight

TWO WEEKS LATER, dressed only in one of Asher's shirts, Emily sipped her morning coffee and tucked her feet beneath her on the linen couch of his 7th Arrondissement apartment with a sigh of contentment. The floor-to-ceiling window across from her was closed due to the chill of the morning air, but it framed a stunning view of the Eiffel tower. She had just finished checking her emails and was enjoying a few moments of quiet.

Asher was in the apartment's office starting his day as he had every day since they'd arrived—by working until noon. Emily didn't mind because it gave her time to answer her own business emails as well as cultivate the new connections she'd made in Paris. She paid bills, contacted artists and collection owners to discuss potential donations, and worked with Mr. Riggins to finalize the long list of what needed to be completed before the museum opened. She didn't want to think about how empty her bank account would be when the project was finished. She preferred to focus on the amount of work she was getting done despite being far away.

Even if it had put her behind schedule, the trip would

have been worth it. The trip she'd thought would last a couple days had stretched into two glorious weeks. Asher had brought joy back to her life. Celeste had been right. Her museum was important to her, but she wanted this, too. She wanted to be young, happy, and free.

There was no better way to describe what the trip had meant to her. She hadn't known what to expect when she and Asher had taken what had started off as a sexual relationship and brought it to the city of love, but he continually amazed her with his attentiveness and thoughtfulness. Their grand tour of the city had begun with the Louvre, where Asher had delighted her by taking her to their tactile exhibit. It was hard not to fall a little bit in love with him because it was obvious he'd planned the trip to please her. They'd spent many afternoons walking through other museums or strolling along the Seine. They ate in restaurants with stunning views and even better food. They ran late to tours and dinner reservations when a simple touch or look had them stripping off each other's clothing with an urgency that showed no sign of abating.

Emily was tingling and alive, and not just sexually.

Paris was more than living up to its artistic reputation. Emily closed her eyes and basked in the memories of where Asher had taken her. *Oh, yes, the Musée National Rodin.* The artist himself had lived a troubled life, but his artwork set a standard few had attained. Her knowledge of his works had been mostly through academic study, but photographs of the experience offered little compared to seeing his sculptures in person. Being in the same room as many of the sculptures that had inspired her was indescribably moving. At the Musée Paul-Belmondo, Emily tried and failed to find the words to express her admiration for the neoclassical, smooth lines of the sculptures. Belmondo was one of her idols, and she was brought to tears of happiness when she discovered a room on the first floor of the museum where visitors were encouraged to touch the replicas of his works. The fact that Asher had shared the experience with her made it that much more meaningful. He was a self-proclaimed art novice, but there were times when he would look at a painting and compare it to what he'd seen in her mother's work or hers, and he would be spot on with his assessment of technique. It was no wonder Asher had become so successful in business. He was brilliant even when taken out of his element.

Just when Emily had thought Asher could not outdo the day before, he had taken her to Le Musée Valentin Haüy, a museum that honored the founder of Europe's first school for the blind. Haüy had dedicated his life to the idea that the blind could learn to read with raised letters, and his ideas paved the way for Barbier, who created a system of raised dots, and Braille, who modified and perfected the system. Asher had set up a tour by the curator, and Emily was able to examine some of the world's first devices for communication for the blind. Her time in Paris brought a deeper awareness of the importance of what she was trying to do in her community: highlight possibilities rather than what had once been called disabilities.

Emily felt herself falling for Asher, and it scared her. Although he had spent every day with her, it was impossible not to ask herself what would happen when they returned home. She didn't doubt that Asher cared for her. He'd filled the last two weeks with immeasurable pleasure, in and out of bed, but there was an invisible wall between them. They avoided discussing the future, the fate of her museum, and how they felt about one another.

No matter how perfect their time together was, they were building a relationship on the uncertain foundation of denial. More than once she'd wanted to ask Asher if he'd canceled his plans for his site in New Hampshire, but she didn't for the sole reason that she didn't want to know if he hadn't. She wasn't ready for her time in Paris to end, and despite the last two weeks, she knew what she had with Asher was fragile. One word. One wrong step and reality would come stomping in to end it. Thankfully, Celeste seemed to understand that. Emily called her every couple days to update her, and they celebrated the wonder of Paris without Celeste asking the questions Emily had no answers for.

A glance at the clock on the wall revealed it was past noon. She closed the laptop beside her, stood, and stretched. As a rule, she didn't bother Asher while he was working, but the news had predicted warmer than normal weather, and she was comfortable enough in the city to go for a walk by herself if he had to work longer that day.

Emily hesitated at the door of Asher's office before knocking. He was speaking to someone and his tone was angry. Emily knew she shouldn't, but she stood there silently and listened.

Asher's voice boomed through the closed door. "Not

possible this late in the game. We've invested too much over there. We have governments all over the region watching to see how we do. I don't have to tell you what a gamble this kind of expansion is. We succeed now, we cement our place in the global market. We fail, we might as well start looking for a domestic bailout."

Emily clasped her hands together in front of her. *Is he talking about Welchton? How could expanding into New Hampshire help him on the global level?* He lowered his voice, and she couldn't understand most of what he was saying, but she did clearly hear him say, "I'll handle this myself."

Handle what?

Emily took a deep breath and told herself not to be paranoid. B&H was a huge company. They were probably expanding into many areas. When Asher had spoken about the possibility of relocating his facility, he had made it sound like an inconvenience rather than something that could threaten financial stability of his company. *No, he has to be talking about something else. He would tell me if he was still moving forward with his New Hampshire site. He said he wouldn't lie to me.*

ASHER WASN'T HAPPY. Although his time in Paris with Emily had been amazing, it couldn't last. There was too much going on with his company back in the US and abroad for him to continue to put off major decisions. He'd known that, but he hadn't wanted to face it. Well, the truth was about to call him.

Thirty minutes earlier, Dominic Corisi's personal assistant, Marie Duhamel, had called and provided Asher with instructions on how to download the Corisi encrypted phone app. It was designed in-house and was supposedly unhackable. Dominic had a reputation for taking security measures to the extreme, but his request didn't bode well.

Asher answered on the first ring. "Dominic, to what do I owe the honor?"

Dominic got right to the point. "My people abroad are concerned with the stability of your site in Trundaie. What's going on?"

Asher leaned back in his desk chair. "Nothing. The imminent risk was neutralized, and we're moving forward with increased security measures."

"You're in over your head, and things are about to get ugly."

Asher rocked forward in his chair. "That's not what my team is reporting."

"Then your team is either stupid, suicidal, or both. My contacts tell me the rebels are amassing weapons for a major assault. They're recruiting mercenary soldiers from Boltatia. The man I gave you doesn't have the manpower to fight that. You have to pull out."

Asher slammed his hand on the table. "Not possible this late in the game. We've invested too much over there. We have governments all over the region watching to see how we do. I don't have to tell you what a gamble this kind of expansion is. We succeed now, we cement our place on the global market. We fail, we might as well start looking for a domestic bailout."

Dominic cut him off. "I'll send you Bennett Stone. He was Special Ops in the Marine Corps. His cousin is my head of security, Marc Stone, and Ben came to work for me when he left the service. You won't find better than either of them. He can keep your people alive long enough for you to pull out."

Dominic's intrusion into the dealings of B&H, along with how his view on things in Trundaie differed from what Asher had been hearing, confused and angered Asher. "I'm not pulling out and, although I appreciate your offer of help, I'll handle this myself."

Dominic swore then said, "Once a month I have dinner with Victor Andrade and your cousins. Maybe you don't give a shit about that side of your family, but they care about you. They see you following in my footsteps, so to speak, and they're worried. I promised them I'd watch out for you."

"I have everything under control."

"Bennett Stone will be in Trundaie by tonight."

Asher shook his head in disbelief. Dominic was crazy if he thought Asher would let anyone handpick his team for him. "If I wanted a Marine to head my team, I'd hire my brother."

"Would you ask him to take a bullet for you? Because that's how ugly Trundaie is about to get. That situation will explode, and if you won't pull out, then you damn well better surround yourself with people willing to die for you, because that's what you'll be asking them to do."

Asher was silent for a moment. He had been in, and worked his way out of, politically sticky situations in the past. Rebels weren't unique to Trundaie. He'd faced his share of them and won. He didn't allow himself to consider failure, and that had always carried him through. This was the first time, though, that he was dealing with such a volatile opponent. Money usually paved the way to a truce. When that failed, a show of force had always proven an effective deterrent. However, if these rebels had seen his show of force as a call to arms, he might need every resource he could gather—even those sent by a side of his family he never spoke to. Asher considered himself a man who didn't need anyone, but if Dominic Corisi was offering to watch his back, he wouldn't let his people be slaughtered because he was too proud to accept the help.

"Tell Stone I'll be in Trundaie by tonight. Have him contact me when he lands."

"Done," Dominic said. "Oh, and Asher—"

"Yes?"

"Don't fly in on your own plane. When your enemy is taking aim, it's best not to wear a bullseye." With that parting piece of advice, Dominic hung up.

Asher made a few phone calls to organize his travel then tucked his phone in his pocket and stood. His mind was already racing as he put together a plan of action for the next twenty-four hours. He would meet with his team, Dominic's man, and a couple of his local contacts who refused to speak to anyone but him. If things were as bad as Dominic thought, his security would require massive expansion. Asher had connections that could handle it, but it would mean calling in favors he'd hoped he never would have to use.

He walked over to the door of his office and hesitated before opening it. Emily was his, and the last two weeks had proven she was meant to be. She would have to understand there were parts of his life he didn't want her involved in. He couldn't take her with him; it was too dangerous. He also couldn't say where he was going; any leak of information could get his people killed. He'd tell her he had urgent business to attend to, and she was welcome to stay in Paris until he returned.

That would have to be good enough.

Chapter Nine

EMILY'S ENJOYMENT OF her walk through the Parc Monceau, a public park she had first fallen in love with through the paintings of Claude Monet, was diminished by the memory of the conversation she'd had with Asher an hour earlier.

He had opened the door of his office and frowned when he'd seen her there. For a moment she'd thought he might accuse her of listening in, but he didn't. Instead he said, "I'm flying out in less than an hour."

"Where are you going?" she'd asked.

"It's work related."

"How long will you be gone?"

He pulled her into his arms and kissed her forehead. "I don't know."

Emily stood tensely in his embrace and tried to keep her voice calm. "Is there anything you can tell me?"

He ran his hands down her clothed back, past the hem of his shirt she was wearing, and up to cup her bare ass. "I don't want to leave you," he murmured against her cheek.

Emily fought the desire that welled within her. One

touch from him and it was too easy to forget everything else. She had to keep her head. She ran a hand over the buttons on his shirt. "I could go with you."

His hands ground her forward against his arousal. "If I could take you, I would." He kissed her neck from ear to shoulder. "If I could delay my flight at all, I'd do that too." He set her back from him with a groan. His eyes were burning with the same desire he'd lit within her. "I can't." He bent and gave her a brief kiss on the lips. "I have to leave—now."

Emily pressed her lips together unhappily, then said, "What do you expect me to do? Sit around and wait to see if you come back?"

He'd pulled her roughly into his arms again and kissed her deeply until Emily clung to him. Usually she welcomed how his touch reduced her to a quivering mass of sexual need, but that was when she was confident her touch did the same to him. This time he was using it against her—to silence her—and although she was turned on, she was angry, too.

When he lifted his head, he grumbled, "I won't be gone long, and I want you right here when I get back." He ran a hand over her thigh and up between her legs to her bare sex. "This wet and this ready for me."

Emily shook her head even as her eyes half closed with pleasure as he circled her clit with his middle finger. "Tell me where you're going. You owe me that much."

He slid a finger inside her and pumped it in and out. "I owe you nothing," he whispered in her ear. "But you'll be here when I return because you're mine, Emily." He worked his fingers magically back and forth over her aroused clit and in and out of her. "You're angry with me, I know, but your body doesn't care, does it? I wish I had time for more, but why don't you come for me before I go, Emily? I want to hear that sound you make when you can't hold back any more."

A part of Emily wanted to fight the hold he had over her. She told herself she should pull away from him, tell him she deserved answers, and that she belonged to no one. The words never left her lips, though, because her traitorous body was humming beneath his touch, clenching and warming as he brought her closer and closer to climax.

He claimed her mouth again, and his passionate demands only made it sexier. With one hand he kneaded her ass, then came around to cup her breast. Their two weeks together had made him an expert on what she liked. He used his knowledge against her in a pleasurable assault that had her writhing against him and crying out into his mouth as she orgasmed.

She slumped after her release and he picked her up, carried her to his bed, and laid her down across it. His shirt was up around her waist, leaving her sex parted and exposed to him. "That's what I want to return to."

The man she'd spent the last two weeks with was gone and in his place was the arrogant wolf she'd first encountered. Emily sat partially up and pulled the shirt down to cover herself. "You can be a real bastard sometimes, Asher."

If she'd expected him to deny it, she was disappointed.

He'd leaned down, given her a quick kiss, and said, "If I wasn't already late I'd spend the afternoon reminding you why you're willing to overlook that about me. I have to go, though. Stay here. I'll call you when things settle down."

With that, he'd left.

Just like that.

Emily stopped and sat on a bench beside the classical colonnade that partially encircled a small pool of water. *Am I a fool to think he cares about me at all? How could two of the most amazing weeks of my life end with me wondering if I know him at all?*

"I want you here, waiting for me, just like that."

Of all the arrogant, sexist things to say. I should have told him what I thought of that comment as soon as he said it.

But no, I was too busy trying to gather my thoughts.

I should not let an orgasm, even a really, really amazing one like that, stop me from speaking my mind.

Emily sighed, stood, and began the walk back to Asher's apartment. *He talks to me that way because I let him.*

Emily blushed. *And because I think it's hot.* She wrinkled her nose as she remembered the night he'd ordered her to strip for him, and she'd admitted to him that she couldn't resist him when he spoke to her that way. *That's what honesty in bed gets me. I had no idea, though, that I could be angry with him and still be that turned on.*

Her complex mix of emotions made her wish she were back in her studio where she would have tried to capture that feeling in clay. Two women in one body: the wary warrior and the joyful lover, both equally strong, and equally capable of being wrong.

She waited for him to call her that night, but he didn't. She picked up her phone again and again to check for a text message that never came. She went to bed, slept restlessly with her phone beside her, and woke angry. As she made her morning coffee, she thought:

He said he doesn't owe me anything. Well, his actions exactly verify those words.

Maybe he's somewhere where he can't call me.

No, see, that's the overly nice side of me that Celeste calls unrealistic. Wherever he is, he could send a text or contact me somehow—if he wanted to.

He didn't trust me enough to tell me where he was going.

He doesn't care enough to call me. I should have trusted my instincts about him.

But then I wouldn't have had these last two weeks.

Two spectacular weeks. Maybe nothing that good can last.

Emily took her coffee to the couch and sat down. The view of the Eiffel Tower only saddened her. She found her sketchpad and pencil and drew her most vivid memories of the trip. Every great artist found inspiration in both beauty and in pain. Emily tried to capture both in her sketches. She drew herself and Asher entwined in a lover's embrace. She drew herself alone and captured the battle raging within her. Her grandfather had believed that joy was fleeting unless recorded by an artist in some fashion. She wanted to keep a piece of Paris with her forever.

One sketch led to another, until she was furiously putting her emotions down on paper. She drew the arrogant

Asher. The tender Asher. She combined the two and saw the man she loved.

Love.

I'm in love with a man who won't even call me his girl-friend.

Who am I kidding, he won't even answer my phone calls.

Did I misread our time together? Was I so lost in the wonder of how it felt to me that I somehow missed it wasn't the same for him?

She drew herself—full of love and tormented by questions—then shed a tear when she looked down into her own face. The tear smudged a part of the drawing as Emily wiped it away.

She was starting a new sketch when her cell phone rang. She answered it absently, "Hello?"

"Emily, it's Sophie Barrington. I hope this is an okay time to call."

Emily closed the sketchpad as if there were a chance Sophie could see it. "No. I mean, yes. I can talk now. You're not interrupting anything."

"When I didn't hear back from you I was afraid my son had scared you off from our family."

Emily pulled her feet up onto the couch and hugged her legs. "No. No. He was fine. I've just been busy with the museum."

"How is that going?"

Emily closed her eyes briefly. She hated to lie so she didn't. "It's coming along." She wasn't ready to admit to herself that Asher could still be moving forward with the buyout of her property, but there was no way she would say anything to his mother.

"I hope you don't think I'm sticking my nose where it doesn't belong, but I've been thinking a lot about your museum. Do you have patrons?"

Sophie's question hit another sore point. "I used to. It's been difficult to get donations because . . . people look at the properties around mine and they worry I'll sell or fail to make a profit when I open." When they'd met, Emily had been truthful about the state of the surrounding properties since Asher's company had bought them. She had described the now derelict buildings and the challenge of maintaining patrons in the face of the changing community. Emily refused to believe they were right back then and she refused to see it now, but there was no denying the situation was getting worse.

Sophie sounded concerned. "Oh, dear. The Barrington family is known for our philanthropy. We'll gladly become one of your patrons."

Although the money would have made an earlier opening possible, Emily couldn't accept any from Asher's mother. "No. Please. You're very generous, but I could never accept money from you."

"Well, then maybe you'll consider an idea I've had. It's genius, really. I don't know why I didn't think of it sooner."

Emily prepared herself to thank her and refuse whatever Sophie offered.

"I've been showing everyone the painting you gave me and telling them about your sculptures. My friends are all dying to meet you. I have an art auction planned for the second weekend in April. Each year we choose a different charity to donate the proceeds to. This year we're giving to St. Jude Children's Hospital. If you'd like to donate something to the auction, I would showcase it. Please say no if you feel this would be too much to ask, but if you'd trust me with some pieces, I would love to have a Harris Tactile Museum exhibit the night of the auction. Everyone who is anyone in Boston comes to my event. If your collection is as good as the piece you gave me, you'll end the night with more patrons than you'd know what to do with. That's what happens when people discover a project as important as the one you're working on."

Emily was temporarily too overcome with emotion to answer. She wiped a tear from the corner of her eye and tried to think of a reason she couldn't say yes. Besides Asher. He'd left her with no idea of when he'd be back. He didn't deserve to be factored into her decision.

Patrons would mean I don't have to live off Ramen noodles while I pay for the audio tour narrator. I could open sooner. I could afford to advertise and reach beyond the ghost town around my property. This could be what makes everything I've worked so hard for possible.

"How would this work?" Emily asked, wanting to scream yes, but she knew being spontaneous had its rewards and its unpleasant revelations—like being left in Paris alone.

"I'll handle the legal details and have the event planners I use contact you. Then it's a matter of picking pieces you feel represent your museum best and having them packed and shipped. I know the perfect people to pack and deliver your pieces. They'll handle everything from pickup, shipping, setup, to returning everything back exactly as you had it. These people are who the Museum of Fine Arts in Boston calls when they need to move six-century-old artifacts. They're that good."

"Sounds amazing." Emily grimaced and added, "And too expensive for my budget right now."

"Emily, what you're building up in Welchton is beautiful, and I selfishly want to be a part of it. Let me do this for you."

Breathe. "Okay. Yes. Thank you. Thank you so much."

"If you give me your email address, I'll have my lawyer send paperwork over to you today. I don't want to rush you, but I'll need your pieces as soon as we can get them here. We'll need to build displays for them, photograph them for advertising the exhibit. We should probably have something written up for each piece."

Emily started to get really excited about the idea. "With a Braille component to each sign. I was hoping to also have an audio tour, but it hasn't come together yet."

In a warm, almost maternal voice, Sophie asked, "Can I make a suggestion? Why don't you come to Boston and help me plan this? That way it's exactly the way you imagine it. I'd love to see you again and, honestly, this is the time of year when I need to focus on happy things. So, you'd actually be doing me a favor."

Emily chewed her bottom lip. "I do have a friend in Boston I could stay with, and I could send a list of items to ship to Mr. Riggins."

"Oh, are you not in New Hampshire at the moment?" Sophie asked.

"No, I'm . . . I'm . . . traveling, but I could be back in the United States by tomorrow if I can get a flight."

"Traveling out of the country. How exciting. I hope I'm not cutting your vacation short."

"You're not," Emily said awkwardly. "I was preparing to fly back soon anyway."

"Where are you?"

"Right now?"

Sophie laughed. "You don't have to tell me. I'm simply curious. I used to love to travel."

Emily felt ridiculous, and she was awful at lying, so she said, "I'm in Paris."

"I adore Paris. My friends wonder how I could love that city and not speak a lick of the language. That never bothered me. Where are you staying? There are so many wonderful hotels."

"A friend of mine has an apartment in the city." Emily rolled her eyes skyward. *Please don't ask his name.*

"Oh, I like that so much better than a hotel. My son Asher has a place in Paris. I haven't stayed there yet, but I hear it's beautiful. Speaking of Asher, have you heard from him since that initial meeting?"

Emily covered her eyes with one hand. *I can't do this.* "I have to go, Sophie."

"Wait, if it's possible, I'd love for you to fly directly here so we could get the details of the exhibition hammered out.

If you don't have a flight already, I could call Asher. I heard he was over there for business."

"Sophie . . ."

"Yes?"

"Do you know where I am?"

Sophie was quiet for a moment, then she said, "I'm afraid if I say yes you won't agree to let me help you with your museum."

Emily lowered her hand and squared her shoulders. "If you're offering because you think there is something serious between your son and me, you're right, I can't say yes." *I wish I could.*

Sophie cleared her throat. "Asher isn't an easy man to love; you don't have to tell me that, but he has his reasons."

The two sides of Asher began to make more sense to Emily. It was what she'd thought; something had hurt him deeply. One side didn't necessarily make the other a lie. They were both within him. Conflicted, just as she was. "Asher wouldn't want me there with you, and I wouldn't want you to help me because you think I'm important to him." Emily blinked back fresh tears. "I don't think I am."

"That breaks my heart, but I know it's not true. I know my son. He's never called his sister for advice about a woman before you. He took you to Paris because he cares about you and doesn't know how to say it. Every parent fails in some way. There were so many things I should have explained to Asher when he was young. I thought I could hide the ugly side of life from the children. I didn't want to burden them with it, but when I see them close people out I worry that I taught them how."

Sophie's words moved Emily. "I'm not sure what to say."

"Say you'll come to Boston. Spend some time with us, and let's get that museum of yours on the map. Have enough faith in my son to believe that even if he gets upset, he'll come around."

"I don't know," Emily said slowly. She wanted to say yes, just as she wanted to believe in Asher. Both were scary leaps of faith.

He's said nothing about what he feels about me. He enjoys me sexually, and we actually have a lot of fun together—even if he can't tell jokes. But he doesn't want more than that, and I'm a fool if I let myself forget that.

"Your visit would make me happier than you could ever know. This a difficult time of year for me, and I was serious that I need to keep myself occupied with good things. If you don't end up with my son, Emily, it won't change how much I want to see you succeed with your museum. Let me do this for you."

"I'll pay you back, Sophie. Once my museum is stable, I'll reimburse you for everything this costs you."

"We'll talk about those details later when you're here. Why don't you pack your things and I'll have a driver come around to pick you up in a couple hours."

Emily shook her head. "I don't have a ticket back yet."

"I'll have everything ready for you by . . . let's say one o'clock. Try not to sleep on the flight back because it'll be early evening when you arrive here, but I'd wait to sleep. We'll send you out for a quick walk when you first get here and reset your internal clock. That's my jet lag secret."

Still feeling stunned, Emily said, "I don't know how to thank you for this, Sophie. It's more than I ever imagined anyone would want to do."

She could hear Sophie's smile in her voice. "See you when you get here. Emily. I just had a wonderful idea. Why don't you stay with us while you're here? The house is so empty with everyone gone."

"I—I . . ."

"Perfect, I'll have a room made up for you. Dale loves to have company. Don't ask him about his golf game, though, or he'll talk your ear off. I can't wait to see you, Emily."

THE NEXT DAY Asher closed the door to his office in Trundaie and sat down on the couch across from his desk. He leaned forward and laid his head in his hands. He was exhausted, frustrated, and for the first time in his career uncertain of what his next step should be.

He'd met Bennett Stone the night before, and Asher was glad he'd *agreed* to add him to his team. Bennett had the air of a former Special Ops Marine, but he was also surprisingly high-tech. He set up a base of operation in the office across the hall from Asher with monitors that displayed both live satellite feed and drone surveillance videos.

He hadn't come alone. The fifteen men he'd brought with him were plainclothes men with earpieces that allowed them to stay in regular contact. He stationed ten of them around the facility and sent five out into the surrounding area. The first twenty-four hours had been devoted to gathering intel.

Asher's meeting with Bennett regarding the findings hadn't been good. Dominic's sources had proven more reliable than his own. The rebels were hiring mercenary soldiers and an attack was imminent on his facility.

"How invested are you in this location?" Bennett had asked.

"Too invested to pull out now," Asher had answered.

Bennett had shaken his head slowly and said, "How far are you willing to go to defend it?"

It was a chilling question, and one Asher hadn't faced before. He had worked with countries with unstable governments before, but things had never progressed to this level. "What lengths are we talking about?"

Bennett had met his eyes calmly as if he were setting the terms for a car purchase. "I'll kill any man who steps onto this facility without permission. I'll take the fight to where these rebels hide, but I won't kill women, children, or innocents. If you need a real war, I can give you names of men who will do anything for the right price. Otherwise, we do it my way. Understand though, that weeding out the trouble from those they entwine themselves with can be tricky and time-consuming. A blunt blanket show of force is initially more effective, but in my opinion politically not advisable. That kind of blood on your hands doesn't wash off easily."

Holy shit.

"I'd prefer we keep the killing to a minimum," Asher had said. Even as he'd said the words they hadn't sounded real.

He'd built his financial empire by crushing his *financial* opponents, but this was different. This involved people's lives. "How dangerous is it for the men and women working here?"

"On a scale of one to ten? Twelve. You picked a tough country to do business with."

"Can you stabilize the situation or not?"

"How cooperative is your contact in the local military?"

"It mirrors how well I compensate him."

"Be generous, we'll need him. I'll organize an initial strike, but it'll have to look like a government action to optimize its effectiveness. We'll scare these bastards where they sleep and spread the word that aligning with rebels is a deadly decision."

"Could this be done without casualties, on either side?"

"Sure," Bennett had said with a half-smile twisting his lips, "if you close up and fly everyone out tonight." Before he'd left Asher's office he'd added, "You don't have much time to decide. I'll be next door when you do."

Asher leaned back against the couch and stared at the wall behind his desk. He could have chosen a safer country to partner with, but the profit margin would have been considerably less. The Prime Minister of Trundaie was gambling that working with an American company would solve their impending economic crisis. As a small country that had aggressively gone through their natural resources, they needed a partnership with a sustainable export. Once B&H had the facility up and running, Asher's people would be slowly phased out and the facility would belong to and be run by Trundaie. The proposed payout would be in the billions and surrounding countries were already lining up to sign with B&H if Asher could pull this off.

He called his business partner on the encrypted wireless line Bennett had installed. "Brice, we need to talk." Normally, Asher let Brice live in the bubble of his laboratory, but Asher's next decision would affect both of them, as well as the future of their company. He updated Brice on the situation in Trundaie and the choices they were faced with.

Brice was uncharacteristically quiet for several moments after Asher finished speaking. "Neither outcome is acceptable."

"No shit," Asher said and rubbed his temple. He hadn't slept in forty-eight hours and his head was throbbing.

"I'm running scenarios in my head. Your present reactants will not result in a product that aligns with our vision for the company. Despite the variable of unpredictability you've described, the answer is simple."

"Now in English, Brice."

"Reconsider your process and each component of it. Remove the unacceptable and reconfigure with a substitution. Your brother Ian has a background in negotiating with countries. He has a skillset that could be the third option you haven't considered. Perhaps a more diplomatic approach could convince the Trundaie government to step up in this situation. The rebels are their issue, not ours."

"My brother. He's never shown any interest in working for B&H."

"Have you ever asked him?"

"No."

"Make that call your next."

The more Asher thought about it, the less trapped he felt. "You're a fucking genius, Brice."

"I know," Brice said in a deadpan voice. "Now, do you have another question or can I get back to my work?"

Asher called his brother next. "Ian, how do you feel about coming to Trundaie and risking your life for a good cause?"

"Are you serious?"

Asher spent the next hour outlining the situation to Ian. He didn't hold back any part of it. Regardless of how they frequently differed in opinion, he trusted Ian with his life. He hoped Ian felt that trust because he was asking him to do the same. "I won't lie; it's dangerous here, Ian, but if you think you can do this, I need you." Those final words hadn't come easily to Asher and a long silence followed them.

"I'll be there tomorrow morning," Ian said.

"You understand how this needs to remain confidential, even within our family," Asher stressed.

"I understand." Before he hung up, he added, "Asher, you've got a reputation for being ruthless. I'm glad the reality of it has been exaggerated. Men don't always come back from what you were considering."

"I know. That's why I called you," Asher said quietly.

After hanging up with Ian, Asher went across the hall and outlined a different plan for Bennett. His brother's safety and that of the people working in the facility were top priority. Bennett's role would be defensive only. Bennett didn't argue, which meant the plan had a potential for success.

A short time later, Asher kicked off his shoes and pulled a blanket out of the closet to throw over him while he cat-napped on the couch. He lay back, closed his eyes, and tried to relax so he could sleep when an image of Emily popped into his mind.

I should call her. He didn't reach for his phone, though. He couldn't imagine what he'd say, and he was too tired to field questions. He let memories of their two weeks together replace the ugliness he was facing in Trundaie.

Paris with Emily had a dreamlike quality to it. He'd stepped outside of his life, away from those who knew him, and had simply been a man spending time with a woman he enjoyed. None of his previous relationships had approached the pleasure he felt simply by being with her. The sex was phenomenal, their conversations were always lively, and when he looked at the world through her eyes he liked what he saw.

She was strong in ways he could admire and soft in ways that brought out a protective side of him. She didn't hide what she thought or try to manipulate him. She was bravely, relentlessly herself, and she inspired him to be more honest with himself about what he wanted both for himself and his company.

If he'd never met her, he might have agreed with Bennett's methods. He'd like to think he wouldn't have, but his father hadn't called him the hammer because he'd spent a lot of time seeking peaceful resolutions to conflicts. He'd never killed anyone, nor ordered anyone killed, though, and thankfully that wasn't about to change.

Asher laid an arm across his eyes and took a deep breath. He could vividly remember every moment he'd spent with Emily. Every touch. Her sweet scent. The contented smile she shyly gave him when she snuggled to his side after sex.

It wasn't easy for him to admit the truth to himself: he missed her.

She wouldn't be happy with him for not calling, but he'd make it up to her as soon as he had the situation in Trundaie stabilized. She was in Paris, and he'd left instructions with Ryan to make sure she had everything she needed. He took another deep breath and fell asleep thinking about Emily and where he would sweep her away to as soon as he returned to her.

Chapter Ten

NINE DAYS LATER, Emily stood in the middle of the climate-controlled storage room in Sophie's ten-bedroom home where over half of the Harris Tactile Museum was now stored in an endless number of crates. The movers had offered to store the crates in a secure location until the event, but Emily couldn't imagine sending her mother's work away, especially since she'd brought so much of it. She'd planned on bringing only a few pieces to Boston for the exhibit, but Sophie had talked her into showcasing the best of what she had. The idea of trusting anyone with the irreplaceable items was terrifying.

Sophie was a soft-spoken woman, probably one of the sweetest people Emily had ever met, but she knew what she wanted and was gifted at working around the word no. *Much like her son.* On the flight over, Emily had planned how she would explain to Sophie that she'd be more comfortable staying with Celeste. Emily remembered starting that conversation, but it hadn't gone anywhere. Sophie had met her in a limo at the private plane she'd hired. She'd taken her home for dinner with her husband, Dale, settled her into a bedroom she'd made up for her, and voila, Emily was staying at the Barrington family home.

When she'd called Celeste to tell her of the change in her plans, her friend had been concerned. "Are you sure this is a good idea?"

Emily had sat on the edge of the bed, shaking her head. "No, I'm positive it's a bad one, but what was I supposed to do? Wait in Paris until Asher came back?"

"Has he called you?"

"No."

"Em, I know I encouraged you to go on this adventure, but it might be time for it to end. You said you had a good time in Paris. Sometimes that's all it is, a good time that only gets ugly if you try to hang on to it after it's done."

"You don't think he was coming back for me?" That idea had occurred to Emily a hundred times already, but she'd pushed it away. He had been too good to her during their time together for her to believe he didn't care about her at all.

"Men are a different than women, Em. Many of them are not really good at expressing their feelings so you have to interpret their actions instead."

"You think it's over?"

"If he hasn't called you, I'm afraid it probably is. Which is another reason why you shouldn't stay at his mother's house. If it's over, Em, you need to go home or come stay with me."

Emily had sighed. "I tried to tell Sophie I couldn't stay here. She's impossible to say no to. And she's helping me find sponsors for my museum. How can I walk away from that?"

"I have a bad feeling about this, Em. Why is she being so nice to you?"

"Because she likes me?"

"I hope that's what it is. You're a good person, so you look for good in everyone. We don't know these people. Be careful."

"If I was careful I wouldn't have flown off to another country with a man I hardly know." As she'd said the words, her voice had cracked with emotion.

"I shouldn't have told you to go. I don't know what the right answers are in these situations. I don't think it's healthy to build your entire life around one goal. I thought if you went to Paris you'd remember what it was like to have fun."

I did. "Celeste, I don't regret going. Yes, it sucks that he hasn't called. Yes, it hurts. But you know what hurt more? Losing my grandfather and then my mother. That's real loss. They loved me. You were right to encourage me to go away with Asher. I needed to step away from Welchton and laugh for a while. Seeing how others have made a difference makes me even more determined to do the same. Sophie said she wants to help me because I'm doing something important. I believe her."

"Call me every day, and let's get together for dinner this week. Text me, and I'll clear my schedule that night."

Coming back to the present, Emily looked around the storage room again. It was packed to near capacity except for a corner where a sofa and a couple of chairs had been put to one side. Even though the men who had delivered the crates had an impeccable reputation, Emily had opened each box and checked the contents upon arrival. Sophie had handled the move professionally and had had her lawyer draw up paperwork that listed each item on loan to her exhibit.

Emily visited the storage room each day and checked on a few of the items. *Like they're family, because they're all I have left of mine.*

Most of her mother's work was there, along with many of the figurines Emily had made for her mother. Emily took out the beach scene she'd shown Asher, sat down on the sofa with the painting on her lap, and ran her hand lovingly over it. *I miss you, Mom. I miss you so much.*

A light knock on the door announced Sophie's arrival. She took a seat in a chair across from Emily. "I knew I'd find you here. Kenzi called and said she's coming to dinner tonight. Grant is too. Would you like to call Celeste? She's welcome to join us again if she's free."

Emily replaced the painting in its crate. "I may go out instead. You and your family would probably enjoy a dinner with only each other for once."

Sophie put her hand on one of Emily's. "You have no idea how wonderful it is to have you here. Kenzi really enjoyed talking to you the other night. She said she'd love to see you again. I told Grant about our goals for your museum, and he offered to help you with the financial planning if you're interested. Every mother thinks her children are amazing, but Grant is truly gifted when it comes to knowing where and how to invest money. I wish he didn't work so much, though. I'll never get grandchildren at this rate."

"I'm sure you will."

"Your friend, Celeste, is single, isn't she? I liked her. Definitely ask her to come to dinner tonight. She might hit it off with Grant. It's a shame there was no chemistry between her and Lance. He needs to find a nice girl."

Emily smiled. "Celeste says she's too busy with her company to think of getting married."

"That's what everyone says before they fall in love," Sophie said with confidence. Her expression turned suddenly sympathetic. "Has Asher called you?"

Emily shook her head. With anyone else the conversation would have been embarrassing, but Sophie was asking because she cared. It was easy to forget she was Asher's mother. Emily straightened her shoulders. "No."

Sophie wrinkled her nose. "I don't know what he thinks is more important than calling either of us back, but when he does, he'll get an earful from me. Ian will, too. He hasn't been answering my calls either."

It was hard to imagine Asher getting a lecture from anyone. "Please don't say anything to Asher about me. It'll be awkward enough when he finds out I'm here."

Sophie studied Emily's face for a moment then said, "Awkward for him, but hopefully not for you. He needs a woman who will put him in his place from time to time. Don't go easy on him when he finally does call you."

Sophie was serious, and that realization made Emily smile. "Aren't you supposed to take his side?"

"He's my son and I love him, but I'm not blind to his

faults. I don't care how old your children get, when you see them acting like spoiled brats you do your best to rein them in. Asher is successful, and he's good-looking. Women have always flocked to him. Frankly, it's given him a big head. He doesn't value anything that comes to him that easily."

Emily blushed a deep red. She'd followed in the footsteps of those foolish ladies. *I gave him what he wanted too easily. Is that why he hasn't called? Is he done but can't be bothered to tell me in person? He'd told me to wait on the bed with my legs spread. Doesn't that exemplify how little he really feels about me? He doesn't call because he doesn't care.*

Loss was something Emily understood far too well. She took her sorrow over Asher and stuffed it deep down into her gut along with her sadness over her mother and grandfather.

Sophie saw Emily's expression and looked instantly contrite. "I wasn't referring to you, Emily. You're different."

Emily looked away. "Not as different as you'd think."

Sophie smiled gently. "Don't be so hard on yourself. You're beautiful, you have a good heart, and you are an amazingly talented artist. That you're humble is a testament to your mother."

Emily's eyes were drawn back to the crate that held her mother's beach painting. "I still miss her so much it hurts."

"I understand," Sophie said. "I lost my parents, my sister . . . my—" She stopped abruptly and stood. "Anyway, Asher is a fool if he doesn't see how good you would be for him. Come on, let's get dressed for dinner."

Emily stood and followed her to the door. She wanted to ask what other loss Sophie had started to mention then decided against it. She paused before turning off the light.

Behind her, Sophie said, "Why do I feel that when the crates move over to the exhibit hall you'll be sleeping there?"

Emily turned off the light and closed the door to the room. "I might."

Sophie put a supportive hand on her shoulder. "I've done plenty of exhibits and even more auctions. We've never lost an item. You can trust me with your treasures, Emily."

TWO WEEKS OF hell passed before Asher was able to fly back to Paris. During the ride from the airport to his apartment, he checked his messages and reflected on how Ian had impressed him. He'd proven that diplomacy had its merits.

A few days earlier, Ian had walked into Asher's office in Trundaie, loosened his tie, and plopped down onto the couch. "I did it. I convinced the prime minister that if he doesn't protect your facility, five years from now he wouldn't have the money for those mega yachts he collects. I also spoke to his advisors about sitting down with the leader of the rebels and resolving the land disputes that started the uprising. Your intel about the rebels was key. Negotiations go much easier when you know what each side wants. They wanted the farmland they'd owned before the prime minister claimed it for another summer home. He's a greedy bastard and had positioned himself as a dictator, but I outlined the cost effectiveness of avoiding a civil war. Once I started talking in terms of who the rebels would come for next, his advisors started listening."

Asher had poured two cups of coffee, handed one to Ian,

then sat across from him. He'd barely slept for over a week. With the lives of his people—and his brother—on his shoulders, Asher hadn't relaxed for a moment until he was certain he could maintain their safety. He'd secured the facility while his brother negotiated with the prime minister. He and Bennett had increased his network of informants as well as paid off several people who swore to stall any act of aggression.

Ian had resolved the situation in a way Asher could live with. Brice had been right: changing one component changed everything. If trouble did come, Bennett was now ready.

He'd thanked Ian, but he doubted his brother knew how much his support meant to him. Trundaie had been the first time he'd found himself in over his head. He'd always known that his siblings would pull together in time of crisis, but watching Ian risk his life to save B&H had reminded Asher of the strength of family.

With the worst two weeks of his life behind him, he could focus on Emily again. At first he hadn't called her because there hadn't been time, but later he'd held off because he didn't want to cloud his judgment with the distraction of his desire for her. He had put everything into saving his company and the facility, and it had paid off.

Asher leaned forward and asked the driver to stop at a florist shop on the way to his apartment. Two weeks without hearing from him couldn't have been easy for Emily. She hadn't answered his phone call or text. He could understand how she might be upset with him, but she wouldn't be for long. He had three days to make it up to her before he flew back to Boston as he'd promised his family he would. Andrew would be home that week and for once Asher wasn't dreading gathering with his family for their annual "pretend Mom isn't too sad to be left alone" week.

After that one week away from her, she could meet back up with him in Boston, or he could return to Paris. He'd let her choose. Now that he was allowing himself to think about her, he couldn't wait to see her again. His mind was pleasantly full of images of the two of them making up for all the time they'd lost over the last two weeks.

He bought three-dozen red roses and spontaneously asked the driver to stop at a high-end lingerie shop. He fantasized not only about what Emily wore, but what he wanted her to wear, and bought enough of both that the sales clerks were smiling and waving at him when he left, which was not a common sight in Paris.

Arriving at the apartment, he carried the roses and one of the boxes. The driver carried the rest. Asher let himself in, placed the flowers on the table, tipped the driver, and frowned. In his last text, he'd told her when he'd be back. Was being out when he returned her way of making him pay for not calling sooner?

He looked around and noticed that her usual coffee cup was not rinsed and by the sink. He walked through to the bedroom and opened the closet. Her clothing was gone.

Emily had left Paris. Irritated and surprised, he walked from room to room and confirmed she had indeed taken everything with her. He called her and was once again put through to her voice mail.

He paced the length of his living room like a tiger confined in a small cage. He'd wanted Emily before, but arriving and not finding her provoked the hunter in him. *Where would you go, Emily?*

He considered using his investigator to track her down, but that would have taken the fun out of the chase. No, he wanted to solve this one on his own. He knew exactly who to call first. "Celeste Smithfield?"

"Yes?" a woman answered warily.

"Asher Barrington. I need to speak to Emily. Is she with you?"

"No."

Asher didn't like the amusement he heard in the woman's voice. "Do you know where she is?"

"Yes."

"Tell me."

To his surprise, Celeste's tone turned cutting. "You'll have to figure out where she is on your own, because if it were up to me, you wouldn't find her. You don't deserve her. Don't call me again." With that, Celeste hung up on him.

What the fuck? Asher glared at the phone. He wasn't used to anyone speaking to him that way, and the more he thought about it the less he liked the fact that Emily hadn't waited for him in Paris. He'd told her he'd be back. He scrolled through his messages and saw an old text from his brother Grant that he'd meant to respond to but he'd put off. He checked his watch, estimating the time difference, then called his brother.

"Asher, where the hell have you been? I was worried until Ian called me yesterday. Neither of you could pick up a phone before then just to tell us you weren't dead?"

Asher sat on the arm of his couch. "We were busy. I had an emergency at work. Ian flew out to help me with it."

"Whatever. I don't care as long as you're here next week."

"I will be. I know how important it is."

Grant sighed. "Good. Hey, in other news, everyone loves your girlfriend."

"My girlfriend?"

"Emily."

"What are you talking about?"

With a chuckle, Grant said, "I didn't know senility set in so young, but have you already forgotten about the woman you sent to stay with Mom and Dad?"

"Emily is staying with Mom and Dad?"

"This work you did with Ian, it didn't involve any brain-altering chemicals, did it?"

"How long has she been there?" Asher demanded.

"About two weeks."

What are you doing, Emily? I thought I'd made it clear I wanted you to stay away from my family. "Do me a favor, Grant, and don't tell anyone you spoke to me. I'll fly in tomorrow, but I'd prefer if no one knew I was coming. I want to surprise everyone."

He hung up the phone and paced his apartment. He was angry, frustrated, and . . . disappointed. It was difficult to admit the last bit to himself, but there was no denying how he felt. He'd expected her to be there.

He'd never done as much to please anyone as he had to please her. How hadn't that been enough? He'd told her he would be back. Why would she leave?

Then he noticed her sketchpad resting against one side of the couch. He picked it up with the intention of flipping through it quickly, but the sketches in it were so emotionally packed that he sat down and turned the papers slowly. There were sketches of him, of her, of them together. Each one brought back memories of their time together with a punch.

Her feelings for him were laid bare in the sketches of herself, along with her anger with him. He wanted to shake her and explain to her that she had no reason to doubt him.

The sketches of the two of them entwined passionately brought his need for her to a painful level. She belonged with him. He had questioned many things lately, but that truth had remained constant.

Emily Harris was his, and he'd prove it to her back in Boston.

Chapter Eleven

T HE NEXT DAY Emily walked Celeste through a huge empty salon. When Sophie had originally told Emily about the auction, she hadn't mentioned it would happen in the Dorvosta building, a well-known location for high-end galas. Sophie and Dale lived a simple life, but they didn't lack for money. That much was clear. "Sophie says this room will be full of chairs all facing a podium that will be over there." She pointed to one end of the room. She said auctions are high-tech now. Some people will be here physically, some will be absentee bidders, and there will even be many people bidding online. I can't wait to see it all in action."

Celeste looked around at the room and whistled. "No one I know could afford to host an event in this room, never mind tie up the rooms that flank it. Your exhibit is happening here, too?"

Emily led the way across the large empty room and tried not to look as nervous as she felt. "Yes, and it spans two rooms. Sophie had everything shipped over two days ago. When I was here yesterday I reminded the workers that the idea is for people to touch the pieces. I hope they understood what I meant. I heard they worked through the night to get it ready for today. Sophie is opening the exhibit for two weeks before the auction. She said that will allow me time to reel in some patrons." Emily stopped at a closed door.

"How much is this costing you?" Celeste asked.

"Nothing. I donated one of my sculptures to the auction and Sophie offered to do the rest. She hosts this event every year. She added my exhibit onto her annual auction." Emily punched in a code to unlock the door then hesitated. "I'm so glad you're here, Celeste. I'm excited and more than a little nervous. This is Boston. Do you know how many museums are just a short walk away from here?"

Celeste's eyes met hers. "You really are nervous. Honey, you've done art exhibits before."

Emily clasped her hands together and admitted, "That was different. Those were usually in my grandfather's old house, and I was telling a story my artwork was a part of. Here I feel . . ."

"What?"

Emily searched for the words to best express how she felt. "Alone. Exposed. My sculptures are good, but they aren't masterpieces. My mother was the true artistic genius in our family. All I did was try to bring paintings to life for her. What if no one gets that? What if my mother's dream ends here—because of me?"

After a brief hug, Celeste pushed the door open, walked in, and gasped. "Oh my God."

Emily rushed after her, looked around, and grateful tears instantly filled her eyes. The finished product was a perfect recreation of how she'd displayed the pieces in her museum. "How did they do this in one day?" She approached one of the displays and touched the Braille and English sign beneath the painting.

Celeste wandered to the next piece. "Sophie is the fairy godmother of auctions, I guess."

The comparison made Emily smile even as she wiped away a tear that had spilled over. She walked from display to display and was speechless in the face of how much care had gone into matching the way she had explained each of her pieces. She stopped in front of a print of Edward Hopper's "Nighthawks." It was a painting depicting three customers lost in their own thoughts at a brightly lit diner. Next to the print was Emily's clay three-dimensional representation of the painting, along with a description of how light and darkness were used to illuminate what many considered an expression of loneliness in a city. Beside Emily's piece was her mother's mono-colored painting that could only be truly experienced through touch. "How am I ever going to be able to thank her enough? This is amazing."

"You may have to marry one of her sons and give the woman the grandchildren she's waiting for. At least they're all good-looking," Celeste said dryly.

Emily's stomach churned as she thought about Asher, but she quickly beat that memory away. "I'm pretty sure it's you she wants to marry into the family. She invites you over every time one of her sons says he'll be there."

"Like I have time to marry. No way." Celeste shook her head at Emily's comment and glanced down at her phone to check the time. "Crap. I have to run. Are you okay?"

Emily looked around the exhibit again in bemusement. "How could I not be? It's perfect."

Celeste gave her a quick hug. "It is perfect, Em. This is the embodiment of what you wanted—to present your mother's talent and vision. Call me tomorrow. I have a client who is going to keep me busy for the next couple of days, but call me. Leave a message if I don't pick up." She waved a hand at the room around her. "Two weeks until the auction?"

Emily nodded.

"I'll see you before then. Bye," Celeste said and left.

Emily stayed and continued to walk from display to display and ran her hands over each one. It didn't feel real, but it was happening. Her mother's dream was becoming a reality.

Two strong arms slid around her waist from behind. She spun and warm lips kissed her neck. She opened her mouth to scream, but the sound died on her lips when her eyes met Asher's. Anger replaced fear. "Don't touch me."

He tucked a wayward curl behind her ear and gave her a knowing smile. "That wasn't what you were saying when I left you in Paris."

Emily slapped his hand away. "*Left* is the key word. I have nothing to say to you."

He grabbed her arm. "That's a shame, because I have a lot to say to you. The most important being, I made it clear I wanted you to stay away from my family."

Emily tried to yank herself out of his hold. When that

failed, she straightened her shoulders and growled. "What you wanted stopped mattering when you didn't call me."

He pulled her against him. "Playing games with me is a bad idea, Emily."

Being near him again set her heart racing wildly. She told herself it was purely from anger. "Doing anything with you is a bad idea. You proved that pretty clearly." She struggled again to free herself.

He took her chin in his hand and held her face still. "God, you're beautiful. I want you so much I could fuck you right here and not care who is watching on those monitors."

Emily clung to her anger, but her stomach clenched with sexual excitement at his comment. She glared up at him and said, "I couldn't be less interested."

He ran his thumb firmly across her lips. "Liar." His eyes burned with a desire that added to the electricity between them. "I want to be angry with you, but I'm so turned on by you that I'm willing to forgive you."

I know the feeling. Emily gave herself an inner smack for wanting him as much as he wanted her. *He's been gone for weeks. One call. One text. And he thinks I'll fall right into his bed? Not this time.*

Even if I want to.

No. No. No. I don't want to.

Wanting is weak. Why doesn't my body get that?

"Get your hands off me," she said tersely, turning her head away from him. "I told you, I'm not interested."

He raised his head and turned, pulling her with him. He closed the door of the exhibit as they left it and kept walking, forcing her to double step to keep up with him. "I would believe you, Emily, but if you never wanted to see me again, you wouldn't be living with my parents, telling everyone we're in a relationship."

Emily dug her heels into the rug and brought them both to a stop. "Your mother asked me to come here. She organized an exhibit for me. I'm here because she is helping me, not because of you. I don't know what she's telling people about us, but I told her we were over."

He glared down at her. "You can walk or I can carry you, but we are not having this conversation here."

"I'm not going anywhere with you," Emily said, raising her chin in defiance.

"Carry it is." He bent to pick her up, but she started walking.

"Oh, I'll have a private conversation with you, but you won't like what I have to say. You have the manners of a Neanderthal. If I ever did find you attractive your behavior cured me of that."

He turned toward her and lowered his mouth until it hovered above hers. "Kiss me and prove it."

Emily took a step back, but he stepped with her. "Why would I do that?"

"Because one of us is wrong, and a kiss would reveal who."

Emily put a hand on the middle of his chest and gave him a shove backward. In surprise he let her go. "You make me so angry I can't think straight."

He held her eyes. "I have a similar issue around you. I

enjoyed our time in Paris very much. I told you I had work I had to attend to. I told you to wait for me. I went to my apartment first. How do you think I felt when I found you'd left, or even worse, that you'd come here?"

Emily pressed her lips together angrily for a moment then said, "I. I. I. Do you know what isn't in what you're saying? Any thought of me and how I felt when you ditched me. How it felt to not know when, or if, you were coming back. Don't tell me what to do or how I feel. There may be an attraction between us, but I don't like you. The next time you lay a hand on me I will do my best to make sure you can't have children. I don't need a kiss to tell me which one of us is wrong. It's you. Talk to me when you can see that."

Emily spun on her heel and strode away from him, tears of anger blurring her eyes. In her haste, she ran full into Dale, who had walked into the room unnoticed.

He steadied her and asked, "Are you okay?"

Dale had been nothing but kind to Emily, and she felt awful as she pulled away from him. "Yes . . . no. I need to get out of here." He let her go, and she bolted out of the building.

ASHER KNEW HIS father had heard too much by the way he folded his arms across his chest and waited for Asher to explain himself. It was a stance he remembered well from childhood but hadn't seen in many, many years. "I should go talk to her."

His father shook his head. "No, you shouldn't. Not yet. Your mother and I have never gotten involved in your business or your relationships, but we like Emily. Right this moment, I like her a whole hell of a lot more than I like my son. You hurt that girl, and you don't care. What does that say about you, Asher?"

Asher's head snapped back beneath the smack of his father's words. "I refuse to discuss Emily with you."

His father gave him a long, hard look. "Why? Because you know you're wrong?"

Anger rose within Asher. "Of course I'm wrong. Everything I do or have ever done in your eyes has been wrong."

Dale's face twisted with emotion. "That's not true."

Asher held his father's eyes angrily. There was no use debating what his father would never acknowledge.

His father sighed and shook his head. "They say children are made from the best and the worst of their parents. You can't see it, Asher, but the reason we butt heads is because you're too much like me."

"I'm nothing like you."

His father raised an eyebrow. "I know what you think of me, Asher. You've always thought I'm weak because I let someone tear down my political career. I could explain myself and change what you think of me, but I'm too damn proud. Always have been. Tell me, who does that sound like?"

Most of Asher's anger dissolved in the face of the raw honesty of their conversation. It was the first time his father had ever addressed the event that had changed all of their lives. "Why didn't you fight for your career, Dad? Why did you just give up?"

"I fought for what was more important, and I've never regretted that decision. Your mother asked me not to take on the one who was spreading lies about me. That's all you need to know. A strong man takes care of those who need him, even when their needs oppose his own. Be the man I know you can be, Asher. Little Emily doesn't need a hammer; she needs a good man who will treasure her. If you can't be that man, I'd like you to go back to Europe until after the auction."

Asher frowned. "Isn't tomorrow the start of the mandatory week with Mom? The one none of us can miss?"

An expression he'd rarely seen on his father's face appeared. It looked like rage. Pain. Before Asher could apologize, Dale rubbed a hand over his temple, then after shaking his head, spoke with controlled anger. "Is that what you consider it? It's not mandatory, Asher." He shook his head again and seemed resigned to be disappointed.

Disappointed in me. Always in me.

In a quieter tone Dale added, "Your mother always feels better when her children are around her during this time, but you shouldn't feel that you *have* to be here."

"I don't understand why you'd want Emily here for a week that has always been about family."

"Your mother enjoys being with Emily. She and Emily have both experienced great losses. I think that's why your mother really wants Emily's museum to work out. She wants Emily to be happy. Your mother is also convinced she'd make the perfect daughter-in-law."

"I have no intention of getting married," Asher said

forcefully.

His father smiled and gave Asher a pat on the shoulder. "Your mother's not picky about which one of her sons Emily chooses. Grant has been helping her organize the finances of her museum. Maybe something will develop there."

Oh, hell no.

His father chuckled at his son's expression. "Your mother was holding dinner until I returned with Emily. If you can bring better than I witnessed here, your mother would love to see you."

Asher thought about everything Emily had said. He was fairly certain he could seduce her back into his bed without changing a thing about himself. Even she'd admitted there was a strong attraction between them. However, he didn't like the man she'd described.

Seeing himself through his father's eyes was even less flattering. Asher would never intentionally hurt Emily. Yes, he wanted her. Yes, he lost his cool around her, but he cared about her. Proof of that was how he couldn't seem to get out of his own way when it came to resolving anything with her.

Without pausing to think about it, Asher knew he could list a hundred things he liked about her. He liked how she saw the world and how he saw it when he was with her. He didn't want to be a hammer if she needed a hero.

With a curt nod, Asher looked back at the exhibit door. He hadn't said a word about it, but he knew how important the event must be to Emily. If he required proof that he was a jackass, it was right there, behind that door. "Dad, do you have the code to get into the exhibit?"

"Yes," his father answered simply.

"Can you give me a tour of it?"

His father smiled broadly. "Gladly."

As they walked through the exhibit, Asher stopped to touch some of Emily's three-dimensional paintings. Like her mother's, they were emotionally charged, honest. They reminded him of the sketches she'd left in his apartment in Paris. "Emily isn't marrying anyone but me," Asher said aloud without meaning to.

His father gave him a pat on the back. "I know, Son. I know."

Chapter Twelve

E MILY WAS THROWING her clothing into her luggage and gathering her things from her room at the Barrington house. She wasn't about to stay in that house a moment longer than she had to. She'd call Celeste on the way to her house. She didn't know what she'd say to Sophie about leaving, but she knew she couldn't stay.

Kiss me and prove it.

I don't have to prove anything to that . . . arrogant, self-centered, egomaniac of a man. I'm glad I told him what I think of him. He's exactly who I thought he was when I first met him. I don't know why I ever let myself imagine he had more to him than that.

The door to her room opened. She didn't turn to see who it was. Sophie was always the one who hunted her down around mealtime. "I'm sorry, Sophie, but I can't stay here anymore."

"Don't leave because I'm an asshole, Emily."

Emily swung around to find Asher standing a foot behind her. If she was hoping he'd look contrite, she was quickly disappointed. He met her eyes with his usual, confident stare. "I'm leaving because you were right: I don't belong here. This is your family, not mine."

Asher sat on the bed beside her open suitcase. "At the moment, I wouldn't put that to a vote."

Emily continued to pack as anger surged within her. "Pardon me if I don't laugh at your jokes."

"The work that took me away from Paris was important and all-consuming."

"I don't want to talk about it," Emily said angrily as she threw things into her bag.

"It wasn't my intention to hurt you."

"Well, you did." She turned to glare at him. "But I've had weeks to get over you, and I have. Now, if we're done, can you go so I can finish packing?"

Asher didn't budge. He studied her for a moment then said, "I had roses with me when I returned to the apartment. Roses and some gifts for you."

Emily paused and put a hand on one of her hips. "Did you honestly think I would be there? After weeks of hearing nothing from you?"

He made a face as if he wanted to say yes but knew it was the wrong answer. "I said I'd be back."

Emily shook out a shirt before folding it. "You told me to stay, but I'm not a dog." Feelings she thought she'd put behind her came rushing back, and she clenched her hands at her sides. "Do you know what the worst part was? I knew what you were like, but when you took me to all those places I never thought I'd actually see and were so damn nice, I thought you cared about me. I thought—" She stopped herself from saying more.

"I do."

Emily bent to retrieve a shoe from beneath the bed and then slammed it into the suitcase. "No, you don't. People who care don't leave you in Paris alone."

"My staff had instructions to make sure you had everything you needed. You were hardly alone."

"Fuck you."

Asher stood. "Well, I can see you're still angry."

Emily looked up at him and her temper soared again. "I am."

They stood nose to nose, both breathing heavily. "What do you want me to say, Emily?"

"Are you sorry about how you left me in Paris?"

"I said I never meant to hurt you."

"But are you sorry?"

"I did what I had to do."

"You can't even say it, can you? What are you afraid of?" She turned her back to him.

After a long moment, Asher cleared his throat and said, "I'm sorry."

Emily looked over her shoulder. "My grandfather used to say, 'Sorry means you'll never do it again.' I don't know if you understand what being sorry really means."

Asher held her eyes. "I've gone after everything I've ever wanted the same way, and I've always won. I don't know how to win with you, Emily."

She turned around to face him again. "That's because we're not on opposing teams. At least, we shouldn't be."

He brought a hand up to cup one side of her face. "I wasn't pretending in Paris. I enjoyed being with you. My company has a facility in Trundaie that was under imminent threat of being attacked. Telling anyone where I was going or what I was doing there could have put lives at risk."

"Trundaie? Aren't they verging on a civil war?"

Asher nodded. "Working with them is profitable but not without risk."

"You could have told me. I wouldn't have said anything to anyone."

"I'd known you for two weeks and lives were at stake."

Emily looked away then back at him. She didn't want to see his point at all and hated that she could. She reminded herself about what he'd said when he'd left her and how high-handed he'd been at the exhibit. A thought occurred to her and she blushed. "How much did Dale hear us say?"

He put his hands on her hips and pulled her gently to him. "Enough to lecture me on my behavior."

Emily folded her arms across her chest, but she didn't pull away from him. "He did?"

Asher hugged Emily to his chest. "He did. And he was right."

Emily stood there tensely for a minute, then relaxed and wrapped her arms around him, and rested her head on his chest. His heart was beating wildly just as hers was. "I still want to kick you in the shin."

"Let's try it later, naked," Asher murmured against her hair.

Emily swallowed hard. She knew if she looked up at him

they would kiss, but her emotions were still too raw, so she simply hugged him tighter. He could have died in Trundaie. The thought twisted her gut. Yes, he had hurt her, and the idea of opening her heart to him again was terrifying, but not half as much as the thought of never seeing him again. In the beginning she'd wondered if her response to him had come from simply craving intimacy with another person; now she saw it for what it was. Right or wrong, in Asher's arms was where she wanted to be.

The door opened after a brief knock, and Sophie walked in. "Oh, good, you two have made up. Which doesn't mean you'll be sharing a room. None of that unless you're married, but I'm happy to see you've worked everything out. Now, come on. Dinner is ready, and everyone is waiting."

AT DINNER, ASHER sat beside Emily and was filled with unlabeled emotions as he watched her interact with his family. The first unexpected realization was that all of his siblings, except Andrew, were in attendance. On a normal week, one or two of them might be there, but full attendance was usually reserved for holidays or the one week each year when they gathered for their mother. It was more, though, than simply the fact that they were all there. The usual underlying tension that made family dinners nearly unbearable was absent.

Asher studied the group as a whole and then individually as he sought the source of the difference. His gaze kept going back to Emily and how her presence appeared to affect his family. His mother was smiling and calm instead of looking emotionally fragile as she normally did during that time of year.

His mother put a hand on his father's arm and said, "And then Emily asked if they were sisters. Cecelia was thrilled, but her daughter stomped off. You know how uppity she can be."

Emily pointed across the table at his brother Lance. "Someone, although I can't say who, told me they were sisters."

Lance sat back in his chair and shrugged off the accusation. "I can't tell Mom's friends apart. Everyone over the age of eighty looks the same to me."

His mother made a mock gasp of outrage. "Neither I nor my friends are even close to eighty. I should make you come to our next bridge club as my partner. Dale, don't you think that would be a wonderful way for him to learn their names?"

Grant coughed and shook his head. "You're in trouble now, Lance."

Without missing a beat, Ian added, "Mom, don't you have a charity ball coming up? I bet dancing with a few of your friends would help Lance distinguish between them."

Kenzi chimed in her idea. "Mom, you love a good auction. You should put Lance up for bid as a dance partner at the ball."

With an impish smile, Emily added, "If the money goes to charity, you have five single sons."

Grant threw his napkin at her and smiled. "You hush."

Emily threw it back. "You don't like the idea? But Grant,

it's for charity."

The easy banter between Emily and Grant sent a stab of jealousy through Asher that he tried and failed to suppress. He placed a hand over hers on the table in a public display of ownership. "Four single sons. One is taken."

He hadn't meant to say it, but once it was out there he wasn't about to retract the statement. He kept his hand on Emily's and tried not to be offended by her shocked expression.

A collective, amused silence fell over the table. If they were waiting for him to say more, they'd be waiting a long time. Asher didn't crack under peer pressure, not even from his family.

Sophie was the first to speak again. "Four it is." A shadow of sadness changed her expression for a moment. "Three really, since Andrew will be deployed again."

Dale took his wife's hand in his. "He'll be here tomorrow. Let's focus on the reasons we have to be happy."

The smile returned to Sophie's face. "You're right." She leaned over and gave her husband a kiss on the cheek. "I don't know what I would do without you."

"And you'll never have to," he answered.

The exchange wasn't an unusual one, but this time it moved Asher. It's always been there—their love—but Asher had seen it as a weakness, not a strength.

In a low voice, Emily said to him. "You're hurting me."

Asher instantly lightened his hold on Emily and met her eyes. He thought about how he'd treated her up to that point and felt an uncharacteristic wave of shame. Emily was a good person, a better person than he'd ever be, and she'd come to him out of desperation. The more he got to know her, the more he learned about himself, and that changed the way he saw her attachment to her museum. It was more than a dream for her; it was also all she had left of her family. Did she feel that she would be alone without it? *I should have helped her. Instead I took advantage of her. My family stepped forward to do what I should have done.* "I won't ever again, Emily. I promise you that."

The dinner plates were cleared away, and Sophie asked if anyone wanted dessert. Asher was impatient to get Emily alone again, but he looked around the table and back at Emily. She was happy with his family, and they were enjoying her. If she wanted to stay, they would stay. He didn't tell her his decision aloud, but they exchanged a look, and he knew she understood.

Emily gave his hand a squeeze and tears filled her eyes. "If your cook made that strawberry tart again, I'm in."

A general agreement spread around the table and Asher found himself in a situation he'd rarely found himself in. He was with his family, choosing to stay longer . . . and he was smiling.

Chapter Thirteen

AFTER DINNER, ASHER asked Emily if she wanted to go for a walk and Emily agreed, but she was nervous. She had no idea what to expect. He'd apologized, and she'd accepted his apology. His behavior during dinner had been proprietorial and part of Emily wanted to tell him she belonged to no one, but a larger part of her wanted to belong.

It was a difficult admission to make. Since her mother had passed, Emily had grown used to being alone, looking out for herself. It wasn't something she'd let herself think about, instead she'd focused on the museum and making it a reality. The past month had been a roller coaster of emotions, but it had also shown Emily what her life lacked—family.

They walked hand in hand through the garden near the house until they came across a gazebo that overlooked a small pond. The sun was setting, but Asher flipped a switch and illuminated the area. "My family seems to really like you."

"I really like them. They're wonderful people. If I tried

for the next hundred years I couldn't thank them enough for how kind they have been to me."

Asher led her into the gazebo, leaned against a railing, and pulled her into his arms. "I've never seen my mother so calm this time of year. Usually we're all walking on eggshells, trying not to say the wrong thing."

Emily relaxed into his embrace. "What happened, Asher? What was so terrible that your family gathers for but won't talk about?"

Asher rested his chin on top of Emily's head and sighed. "Kenzi was a fraternal twin. My parents had planned a trip to Aruba for their anniversary, then found out they were pregnant. Their trip was doctor approved, but my mother went into labor while there. They were premature. Kenzi survived, but the baby my parents named Kent didn't."

Emily leaned back so she could see Asher's face. "How old were you?"

"I was young. Too young to be told the circumstances around what had happened, but old enough to understand that it had changed my family. My mother hasn't been the same since. My father, either. Shortly after they lost the baby, my father's political career was hit by a scandal. The news accused him of supporting a mistress with government funds. He claimed he never cheated on my mother, and she believed him. It's one of the many subjects we don't discuss."

"I can't imagine Dale cheating on Sophie. The way he loves your mother reminds me of how my grandfather loved my grandmother. I never saw them together, but he never remarried. Even by the time I came along, he was still talking about her being the love of his life. When he passed, my mother said it was hard to be sad because she knew he had someone waiting for him at heaven's gate. It wasn't the same for her, but I like to think they're all together now."

Asher hugged Emily closer. He was quiet for a moment then said, "My father gave me a tour of the exhibit after you left. It's remarkable how closely it mirrors your museum."

"That was the genius of your mother and the event planner she hired. I wouldn't have been able to organize anything of this caliber on my own. Not yet."

They stayed as they were, simply holding each other. Emily didn't want to ruin the mood by bringing up the fate of her museum, but it was a wall between them that could no longer be ignored. Even though she tried to sound as if her whole world didn't hinge on his answer, her voice wavered as she asked, "Have you made a decision about your facility in New Hampshire?"

He held her back from him and met her eyes. "I can't see how I could move forward with it now."

Relief flooded through Emily, but it was quickly followed by a need only he could fill. His hunger for her lit an equally consuming one in her. "You're not angry with me for being here with your family?"

He framed her face with his hands and caressed her cheeks lightly with his thumbs. "Anger is not at all what I'm feeling right now."

Emily tipped her head back and closed her eyes in anticipation of his kiss. Despite the coolness of the night air, her skin was warm and tingling, eager for his touch. He gave her a tender kiss instead of the hot assault she'd expected. When he broke off the kiss, her eyes flew open in confusion. She searched his face for a hint of what he was thinking. He wanted her, but he was holding himself back. "What's wrong?"

He chuckled and kissed her forehead. "My parents' garden is hardly the place for what I want to do with you."

Emily looked around. When she was with him it was too easy to forget everything else. Her cheeks warmed with embarrassment. "Of course, I wasn't suggesting—"

He hugged her to his chest. "Never be embarrassed with me, Emily. I love your honesty, your openness. I hope to hell what you feel around me is as good as what I feel around you. Most of the time I want you so badly, I can't think. If you don't believe me, listen to the idiotic things that come out of my mouth whenever you're around. I've never threatened to carry a woman off anywhere, but you bring out a side of me I didn't know existed."

Emily blushed again, but this time for an entirely different reason. Her mind flooded with images of their bodies intimately joining again and again. "I shouldn't tell you this, but that was pretty sexy, even though I was too angry with you at the time to want to go anywhere with you."

He groaned. "I'm trying to do the right thing here, but now all I can think about is dragging you to my apartment and making love to you all night."

Emily licked her bottom lip. "I'm not angry anymore."

He set her back from him and took a deep breath. "You accused me of being a man who thinks only in terms of what

I want. I don't want to be that man. Everything else aside, this is the week my family comes home to support my mother. Andrew will arrive tomorrow morning. I should be here." He ran a hand through her hair. "You should be here, too. What we want can wait one week. I have work I need to do even while I'm here, but next week, everyone leaves; come back to my apartment in Boston and I'll take some time off. We'll celebrate your exhibit all day and all night long."

Emily had glimpsed this side of Asher before, but there was a new look in his eyes that had her heart beating wildly and her mind racing. The artist in her paid attention to detail, sought to capture expressions by understanding the emotions behind them. *He looks like a man who is falling in love.*

Panic rose within her. *Isn't this exactly what happened in Paris? I wanted more than he'd said, so I imagined it was there in the way he looked at me, in the way he treated me. But it wasn't. He. Left. What if it's not there now?*

"Are you ready to go back?" Asher asked and took her hand in his.

She knew he meant back to the house, but the question elicited a strong response within her. A few hours earlier, she'd been packing her bags with the intention to leave. She hadn't allowed herself to think about what she'd be walking away from. *I don't want to go back to New Hampshire yet. I'm happy here.*

What is wrong with me? Everything that's important to me is in Welchton.

Or is it?

Asher, how can you give me so much and so little? She wanted to grab him by the shoulders and demand answers to the questions relentlessly ruining what would otherwise have been a romantic stroll. *Are you serious about me? What happens after the exhibit? Are we building something together or back on the wild, temporary ride to nowhere?*

Asher touched her face. "Is something wrong?"

Emily lied with a shake of her head.

Yes, I shouldn't be in love with you.

But I am.

SEVERAL DAYS LATER, Asher woke alone in his bedroom at his parents' house with a smile on his face. Life was good. Things were under control at work, and he was clearing his schedule for the next week. *One whole week of Emily. Just Emily.* He should have been tired from doubling up his meetings and forcing his normally longer days into a nine-to-five workday, but he had never felt better.

He and Emily had spent every evening with his family in one fashion or another. They stayed in for a welcome home family dinner for Andrew. They'd opened Emily's exhibit to the public and spent several evenings there, meeting the first exclusive wave of those his mother had invited for special viewings.

He thought he'd admired Emily before, but watching her hold her own with both the hard-to-impress art elite as well as those who made their living by critiquing the work of others, brought his admiration to a whole new level. She didn't waver before their questions. Her belief in the importance of her collection and her dream shone through whatever nervousness she claimed she had. He wasn't surprised when his mother reported that most who attended the exhibit were prepared to commit to some level of patronage. The younger philanthropists wanted more details on how the money would be spent before signing their checks, but, according to his mother, that was the trend every museum was facing. Her generation had given for the accolades and saw it as an investment in the arts. The younger generation felt divided between the arts and social causes. They were harder to win over, but generous once they had been.

Asher offered Emily a generous donation, but she refused it. She said she wanted to do this on her own, and he respected her more because of it. While watching her walk people through her exhibit, it was impossible not to want her to succeed. His stomach twisted painfully every time he considered how close he'd come to taking it away from her. He wanted Emily, but even more than that, he wanted to see her dream become a reality.

With that in mind, in a meeting with his team who had been working in New Hampshire, he told them he would be buying the lots from his company and making the project a personal one. Until that phase was completed, he wanted them researching and pitching alternate sites.

Asher rolled onto his back and sighed. Like every other morning that week, he'd woken with a throbbing erection. Although he was enjoying the week with his family more than he had in a long time, he was looking forward to having

Emily all to himself. Waiting to be with her again was excruciating, but it had also taught him something.

He'd never put much thought into the differences between the casual affairs he'd had with women and what his parents had, but he saw it clearly now. His personal goals were still paramount to him, but Emily's happiness affected his own. When she was laughing and smiling, he was filled with unexpected warmth that made every moment of his day more vibrant. Colors were brighter. Food tasted better. When he breathed in, he felt lighter.

He imagined the pleasure he would find in just a few days when Emily would be beside him in his bed. He would leisurely claim every inch of her until neither of them could stand, then spend the next day exploring the limits of their sexual stamina again. A knock on his door pulled him back to reality.

Ian called through the door. "Asher, are you up?"

Asher looked at the large tent in his sheet and swore. "I'm not dressed. What do you want?"

"We need to talk before you head off to the office. Meet me in the library."

"I'll be down in fifteen minutes." *After a very cold shower.*

Asher threw back the sheets, stood, and stretched. He checked the clock beside his bed. He had time before his first meeting. Hopefully whatever Ian wanted to discuss would be brief.

A short time later, Asher entered the library and saw Ian standing beside the lit fireplace. "I don't have long, but what do you need?"

"Close the door."

Asher raised one eyebrow in surprise then closed the door behind him. It wasn't like Ian to be secretive. He studied his brother's face. Something was wrong. Something serious. Asher walked across the room and stood in front of the fireplace. "What's going on, Ian?"

Ian looked Asher over from head to toe then said, "I want to make sure we're all on the same page about Emily."

Asher's jaw tightened in preparation of a conversation he knew wasn't going anywhere good. "And what page would that be?"

"Having Emily here and raising money for her museum has given Mom something good to focus on. We were all talking, and we don't want anything to threaten that."

Folding his hands over his chest, Asher narrowed his eyes and asked, "Stop dancing around what you want to say, Ian."

"Don't buy Emily's land. Don't demolish her grandfather's house. I know that when it comes to business for you, profit always comes first, but this project needs to happen. If your money is tied up abroad, and you can't afford to relocate your facility, tell me and we'll figure something out. Between us, we easily have the liquid assets to cover what you'll lose."

It bothered Asher that his family had seen him with Emily and still thought he would move forward with his facility. "And what would you all do with half a town in New Hampshire?"

Ian ran his hand through his hair in agitation. "I don't fucking know, Asher. I'm hoping it doesn't come to that. Is it going to come to that? With you, I honestly can't tell."

"That's a wonderful opinion you have of me."

Ian let out a long breath but said nothing.

A memory of something his father had said came back to Asher. *"I could explain myself and change what you think of me, but I'm too damn proud. Always have been. Tell me, who does that sound like?"* Asher slammed a fist against the wall. His family mattered to him. Emily mattered to him. He'd spent most of his life trying to be the opposite of his father and didn't like discovering he was following in his footsteps. "I'm already actively seeking another location for my facility. So tell the family they don't need to save Emily from me."

Ian's stance relaxed. "Thank God. It's not just Mom everyone is worried about. Emily is a nice woman. No one wants to see her hurt."

Asher tensed again. "What is that supposed to mean?"

"You know how you are. Don't be that way this time."

Ian's words echoed in Asher's head. '*You know how you are. Fuck. Is this how they all feel about me? Don't be* that *way this time. Do they all see me as an uncaring, ruthless bastard? Even Kenzi?* The thought made Asher even angrier, even if he didn't know who he was most angry at.

Asher glared at his brother. "As enlightening as this conversation has been, I have an early meeting this morning. Is there anything else you needed to get off your chest?" Ian opened his mouth to say something, but Asher raised his hand. "I was joking, I really don't want to hear it."

With that, Asher turned on his heel and strode out of the library. He was angrily shrugging on his jacket when Emily appeared.

She read his mood and instantly looked concerned. "Is everything okay?"

His feelings for her rose and mixed with the anger he still felt toward his brother. He wasn't the man he'd been before he met her, and the change in him was something he was slowly working through. If his family was still worried he would destroy her dream, did she have the same fear?

If so, what could he say that would make her see how he felt about her? That was the moment he realized something that rocked him back onto his heels. *I want this to last. I want Emily in my next week, next month, forever.*

He swung her up into his arms and kissed her deeply, passionately, momentarily letting go of the control he'd maintained all week. She met his kiss with a passion that matched his, and had they been anywhere but the hallway of his parents' home, they would not have remained clothed long. "Emily, I—"

Kenzi made a loud announcement from the doorway. "No, Mom, Asher must have already left for work. He's not in here."

He looked up in time to see Kenzi turn away. This wasn't the time or the place for what he'd been about to say. "Emily, let's go to dinner tonight. Just you and me. There's something I need to tell you."

Looking adorably flushed, Emily breathed raggedly and asked, "Didn't we promise a Scrabble rematch with Andrew and Grant tonight?"

"This is more important," Asher assured her. He gave her

one final quick kiss and promised to be back as early as he could. He paused before walking out the door and said, "Pack an overnight bag for tonight." The answering flare of desire in her eyes was all the yes he required. Although he'd said they should stay at his parents' house all week, one night away was needed. When he told Emily how he felt about her, he was certain she'd agree.

Chapter Fourteen

EMILY SAT ACROSS from Asher in easily the most expensive restaurant she'd ever eaten in. The food came in tiny, decorative portions that normally wouldn't have satisfied Emily, but her stomach was a bundle of nerves, and she had barely tasted the first two courses. They'd successfully talked about nothing in particular to that point.

Asher reached across the table and took her hand in his. "I'm glad you decided to stay."

The warmth in his eyes took Emily's breath away. She bit her bottom lip to hold back the nervous babble that threatened to spill forth. "Me, too."

"Not quite Paris, but this has been good."

"I agree."

"You seem to enjoy Boston."

"I do."

"The support for your project has been substantial."

"It's been amazing."

"Imagine the traffic your museum would get if it were here."

Emily took a quick sip of water and choked. Was he saying he had changed his mind and was moving forward with the facility? When she could speak again, she said, "What are you saying, Asher?"

He turned her hand over and lightly caressed the inside of her wrist with his thumb. "If you moved your museum here, you wouldn't have to leave after the auction."

Emily's heart started beating wildly. "You know I can't do that."

He laced his fingers with hers. "Can't isn't in my vocabulary. It never has been. When I want something, I assess what is standing between me and what I want, then remove the obstacle. What is stopping you from saying yes to me?"

The warmth she'd seen in his eyes earlier was replaced by determination. On one hand it was a dream to know he wanted her to stay, on the other hand he wasn't declaring his love for her. He wanted her with him, but he wasn't giving her more than that. "What are you asking me to say yes to?" Although she'd never judged her mother for her decisions, Emily wanted more for herself. Was Asher able to give her that?

"I don't want you to leave after the auction."

"You know I have to go back, Asher. If I get the funding your mother thinks I will, I can finish the museum ahead of schedule. I'm so close. I need to be there for the final phase."

He took out a folder and handed it to Emily. "Most of your pieces are already here. I found a building in Brookline that would be perfect for your museum. You don't need to rely on donations to renovate it. I'll back your project. In my estimation, we could have the place ready in less than two months."

Emily gripped the folder in her hand for moment. She didn't want to believe he was still hoping to buy her land, but she had to know. "And what would happen to my grandfather's house? To my land?"

"We'd figure that out later."

Acid churned in Emily's stomach. "My grandfather's house is where I grew up. It's where my mother and I envisioned the museum, and it's where it has to be." She handed the folder back to him unopened. The magic of the days they'd spent together with his family faded. "That hasn't changed." *Please tell me it doesn't matter, that all you really care about is me, and figuring out how we can be together.*

Asher frowned. "If you stay here, I'd want you to move in with me."

"For how long?" Emily asked, no longer able to hold in her fears. "Until you convince me to sell my land?"

He reached for her hand, but she clasped them in front of her. "I don't care about your damn land."

Emily stood. "Well, at least you're honest about that. Take me back to your parents' house, Asher."

Asher slapped several large bills on the table and walked out of the restaurant with her. As soon as they were outside he swung her toward him. "Most people would be grateful—"

"Grateful? You're lucky I didn't take that folder and stuff it up your—"

His kiss cut off the rest of what she would have said. She fisted her hands at his shoulders and hit him, but her anger quickly sparked into desire as her body leapt to life beneath his touch. She was angry, but that didn't stop her from opening her mouth to him, clinging to him. No matter what else was between them, this was one area where they were perfectly in accord. He backed her against the wall and kissed her until they were both feverishly close to taking it too far, despite being in public.

He raised his head, and between ragged breaths he said, "Let's go."

With a hand on her lower back he guided her to his car. Emily was still trying to gather her scattered thoughts when she realized they weren't headed in the right direction. "Where are we going?"

He shifted his car forcefully and said, "To my apartment."

Despite the way her body was already wet and craving him, Emily resisted. "I said I wanted—"

He shot her a hot glance. "We both know that's not what you want, Emily. It's not what I want either."

Emily closed her eyes and tried to muster a denial to his claim, but the chaste kisses they'd exchanged all week had built a wild need within her. *How can I want him when he hasn't answered my questions? I am worth more than just being his convenient fuck. I want to be loved. To be cherished. He says he doesn't care about my land. If he doesn't care about that, he doesn't care about me. Where is my brain? Why can't I walk away from him?* She opened her eyes and peered over at him. Speaking more to her libido regarding its weakness than to him, she said, "Sometimes I hate you."

He laid a hand on her thigh. "No, you don't. You get

afraid, and I don't help by saying stupid shit when I'm around you. I meant to tell you this week has been one of the best of my life. You're not only great with my family, but everyone is happier because you're here with us. I'm happier. That's why I want you to stay." He rubbed his hand up and down her thigh. "That and I want to fuck you so badly I can't think straight."

His words had her mind racing and her sex clenching with desire. Breathlessly she said, "I loved every minute of being with you this week. I want to say yes, but what happens next?"

"Whatever we want," he ground out when he slowed for a stop sign. The kiss he gave her then wiped the rest of her mind clean of anything beyond wanting to be with him again.

Parking the car at Asher's apartment building and taking the elevator was a blur of feverish, impatient kissing. They started unbuttoning each other's clothing before they were inside the door of his apartment.

Asher slammed the door behind them and continued to kiss her deeply as he stripped her bare. She was completely naked and all he'd shed was his coat. If asked, Emily would have said she was the type of person who preferred to be in control. Like her mother, she'd been raised to be a strong, independent woman. What she thought she wanted and what she found pleasure in were two very different things. Giving herself over to Asher's control should have been scary, but in this area at least, she trusted him. He would demand everything from her, but in return, he would give her more pleasure than she'd ever known. This had never been their problem.

He lifted her so her legs wrapped around his waist. His belt bit into her thighs, but the pleasure of his mouth hungrily kissing her neck far outweighed the pain. He held her to him with one arm, and his free hand expertly went from one of her breasts to the other until both were eager for his mouth.

She dug her hands into his hair and writhed against him, loving the feel of his business clothing against her bare skin but craving the feel of his skin. He turned and walked her a few strides to the dining room table. He sat her on the edge, leaned above her, and cleared the centerpiece with a swipe of his hand. Emily lay back onto the table and spread her legs for him.

He stood there for a moment looking her over hungrily. He sank to his knees between her legs while positioning her at the end of the table. He kissed the inside of her right thigh, then her left. His breath was hot on her exposed sex when he said, "I want to see you make yourself come, Emily. Touch yourself for me, baby."

Emily ran her hand down her stomach and her trimmed sex. She dipped a finger between her lower lips. She was wet and ready for him. She circled her clit slowly, then faster, building a tempo she was well familiar with. Then she stopped, pulled him forward with her legs, and ran her wet finger across his lips. He made an animalistic noise as he lost control and took her sex into his mouth. His tongue plunged inside her while his fingers encircled her engorged clit.

The push and pull of their lovemaking had never been clearer than in that moment. Asher was definitely a man who knew what he wanted and was used to demanding it, but he was as helpless as she was in the face of passion. He teased and loved her sex until she was on the brink of an orgasm.

He replaced his tongue with two fingers and rose to his feet. He dug his other hand into the back of her hair and raised her face to his. Emily tasted herself on his tongue and cried out as he plunged his fingers into her again and again. Deeper and harder until she came with a sob, clenched around his fingers.

She was still in a haze when he stood and stripped. A moment later she felt the tip of his cock rub over her clit. He lifted her hips off the table with one arm and continued to kiss her as he plunged deeply into her. His thrusts were powerful, and each one had Emily gasping as it was almost too deep, too good. There was no escape, but Emily wasn't trying to.

He nipped her neck and moved down to claim one of her breasts with his mouth. There was nothing gentle about the way his teeth pulled at her nipple, but Emily grabbed the back of his head and held him there, begging him not to stop. And he didn't. He easily took her to a second orgasm, and only when she was calling out his name wildly did he give himself over to his.

He pulled out, lifted Emily into his arms, and walked to his bedroom where he laid her across his bed. He was back a moment later with a warm washcloth and wiped her intimately. "Are you on birth control?"

"I think so. I mean, yes," she said, barely able to think in the aftermath of the soul-rocking climax.

He threw the towel across the room into the door of the bathroom. He joined her, pulled her into his arms, then covered both of them with a sheet. "It wouldn't matter. You're mine, Emily. We'll figure everything else out, but you're not leaving Boston."

Emily opened her mouth to argue with him but closed it when she realized she was too relaxed to fight. She was floating in the peaceful sated place she only found in his arms. An hour would change nothing. She rested her head on his shoulder and let herself melt against his side. She'd give herself a few more minutes of bliss, then she'd tell him exactly what she thought of the way he'd spoken to her.

She closed her eyes and inhaled his scent. She didn't want to rehash the conversation they'd had earlier. Not yet. All she wanted was a few more minutes in heaven.

ASHER WATCHED EMILY pretend to sleep and smiled. He knew she hadn't liked what he'd said, but she was too happy with him to say so. It was adorable. *Note to self: multiple orgasms win arguments.*

He absently caressed the curve of her ass and her lower back as he rehashed the night in his mind. He knew he wasn't an easy man to get along with, but he did want Emily to be happy. He understood that her land was important to her. It was why he'd agreed not to move forward with the facility there. That didn't mean, though, that he liked the idea of her living in New Hampshire while he was living in

Boston. He'd hoped she would see his offer to help her relocate to Boston as a declaration that she was important to him.

For Emily he was breaking his own rules. He'd changed business plans for her and had offered to invest in hers. He had never done that for anyone, not even his family. He'd also never asked a woman to live with him before.

He remembered how he'd suggested she should be grateful. He hadn't meant that the way it had sounded. He'd meant she should appreciate the fact that he'd put time and money into finding a nearby location for the museum. He cringed when he considered the pompous ass he'd been. Emily was a woman who would always keep him on his toes and demand better from him. He was beginning to think that was a good thing.

"Emily," he said.

Her eyes opened slowly, and she watched him warily. "Yes?"

"I care about you, but . . ."

She tensed in his arms. "But?"

"But I'm not what people would call a romantic guy. I don't do relationships. I never have. So I don't spout smooth lines. I've always been blunt about what I wanted, and it has always worked out. Women usually want to sleep with me, and it's never been more complicated than fitting them into my schedule."

Emily rose up onto one elbow and looked down at him. "Do you know what a nipple twist is?"

Asher rolled onto his side. "I'm being honest."

Emily nodded but continued to look at him in a way that made him want to protect parts of his body from her. "I know."

He sighed and continued, "Don't look at me like that. I remember telling Andrew he shouldn't join the Marines. He told me he didn't have a choice. I joked that he was born to smash things, kill people, and save the world. He joked that I was born to make money, make more money, and in general be a dick. I've always laughed. I've never cared what anyone thought of me until I met you. How do we always get to this place?"

Emily cocked her head to one side. "Because you speak dick?"

His eyebrows shot up, then he threw back his head and laughed. She joined in, seemingly thoroughly amused by her joke. He rolled on top of her and growled, "I was being serious."

Her expression softened. "So was I. Asher, if you want to be with me, be with who I am, not who you want me to be. I don't need you to give up what's important to you; don't ask me to do that for you."

He ran a hand lightly up her bare arm. "I don't want to change you."

She leaned over and kissed his lips lightly. "Then instead of looking for real estate for me, buy me flowers on the opening day of my museum in Welchton. That's all I want. Can you promise me that?"

"I can." He hugged her to his chest. Her request touched his heart. He was used to people wanting something from him, but Emily didn't care about his money or his social circle. She held him to a higher standard, and as he held her he admitted to himself he could no longer imagine his life without her.

Chapter Fifteen

TWO DAYS LATER Emily was sitting next to Asher on the couch in his parents' living room as Kenzi drew what looked like a lizard on a large sheet of paper. Weeks ago, dinners were always followed by tea or coffee in the living room and serious conversation. The tension had been unbearable for Emily so she'd suggested board games. The Barringtons didn't follow all the rules, but they embraced the idea of making evenings fun. Dale told Emily she'd brought laughter back to his house, and that was why she'd always be welcomed there. Emily still got misty just thinking about it.

"Godzilla," Ian called out.

Kenzi shook her head and put clothing on the lizard.

"It's that gecko from the commercial," Sophie guessed while waving her hand at the picture.

"No," Dale said, "it's an alligator, but why is he wearing clothing?"

Kenzi drew a bell next to the alligator. Then a trash can with broken cans next to it. She tapped the alligator's neck, the bell, then the trash can.

In frustration, Kenzi drew a golf tee and ball after the

alligator and then after the trash can. She tapped all of the items again.

"Time's up," Grant announced. He looked over at Asher, Emily, and Lance. "Does our team have a guess?"

Emily assessed Kenzi's art ability and let her imagination go wide. "I've got it! Humpty Dumpty."

Kenzi clapped. "You got it."

Ian said, "You realize you're clapping for the other team."

Kenzi threw the marker at her brother. "I would clap for my team, but you can't figure out a simple pictogram."

Andrew laughed. "How could anyone get Humpty Dumpty out of an alligator and a bell?"

Kenzi pointed to her first drawing. "That is obviously the hump on the Hunchback of Notre Dame. Why would I put clothes on an alligator?"

Ian sat back and folded his hands over his chest. "Since when does Quasimodo have a snout?"

"If you think you can draw better than I can, why don't you come up here next?"

Ian flexed his shoulders and rose to his feet. "Oh, I will. Wait, isn't it the other team's turn?"

Asher said, "Doesn't matter; we'll probably get the point anyway."

Andrew threw a pillow at Asher, who caught it and threw it back.

Sophie told them all to stop, but she was smiling when she said it. Dale looked over at Emily and nodded in approval. Emily turned to look up at Asher and saw a similar expression in his eyes. Emily spontaneously gave Asher a quick kiss then hugged him. She couldn't remember ever feeling happier.

Her phone rang, and she almost ignored it, but she saw it was from the caretaker of her museum so she said, "Excuse me. It's Mr. Riggins. I'm sure this will be quick." She stood, walked to the doorway of the living room, and answered the phone.

ASHER WAS ON his feet and at her side the moment he heard her gasp.

"Oh, my God. No. No." She looked around the room frantically and her voice rose. "No."

She slumped against the wall and would have sunk to the floor if Asher hadn't caught her.

Asher took the phone from her. "What happened?"

Mr. Riggins said, "The fire department is already here, but they're not sure how much of the building will be left. It was already engulfed in flames when I went to check on it. I did everything I could."

"What are you talking about? What's burning?"

"The Harris Museum. The whole thing is ablaze. I checked in on it as I always do, but it was already too late."

"How did it happen?"

"No one knows yet. The firemen say they have to get it under control before they can determine the source for sure. They keep asking me what I know, but I don't know anything. It's like I said, as soon as I saw the fire I called them."

Asher hung up the phone and tossed it on the table beside him, turning his attention to the woman he was partially supporting. He turned back to his family and said, "It's Emily's museum. It's on fire."

Everyone was instantly on their feet and gathered around her, asking both Emily and Asher the same questions neither of them had answers to. Asher turned his attention to the woman in his arms who was shaking from the shock.

She went to pull away from him. "I have to go."

"I'll go with you," Asher said instantly.

Emily looked up at him and an expression of horror entered her eyes. "You didn't have anything to do with this, did you? Swear to me you didn't."

Asher's head snapped back in surprise. "I didn't do this."

Pale and shaking, Emily looked past him to his family. "I want to believe you. You have all been so good to me, but is this why? Was all of this some sick plan to get my land? You lure me away, have me relocate my pieces, then burn it so I have nothing to fight you over?"

"You can't believe that." Sophie reached out to Emily, but Emily backed away from her.

"I don't know what to believe," Emily said as tears poured down her cheeks. She pushed away from Asher. "Don't touch me. I need to think."

Grant stepped forward. "Emily, no one here would ever hurt you."

Emily swayed on her feet and waved a finger at Grant. "Why did you encourage me to take out more insurance? Did you know this would happen?"

Dale put his arm around Sophie. "She's in shock. She

doesn't mean what she's saying."

Kenzi looked from Emily's distraught face to Asher's and asked, "Did you do this, Asher? Could one of your people have done it?"

Sophie covered her mouth as she gasped. "Asher, tell me there is no chance you could be involved. Even you wouldn't go this far to get what you want, would you?"

Asher opened his mouth to deny it, but he remembered what Ryan had said about Hearne. "I told my team we were pulling out of New Hampshire."

Andrew shook his head. "Did you tell them it was because you fell in love with Emily? I bet you didn't."

Asher met his father's eyes. "I didn't tell them anything. I don't explain myself to anyone. But I told them to look for another location."

Ian interceded. "Let's not assume anything until we have the facts."

As he walked away, Lance said, "The facts look pretty damning."

Emily turned back to Asher. "Would anyone who works for you do this?"

If Asher had been a liar, he would have lied then. "If they did, it wasn't on my orders. I don't condone arson."

Emily sank to her knees and started to sob. Asher tried to help her up, but she pushed him away. His family looked on helplessly, a mixture of sympathy for her and anger at him.

Sophie walked up to Asher, tears in her eyes, and laid a hand on one side of his face. "If you did this, Asher, you went too far. You. Went. Too. Far."

Dale led her out of the room.

Kenzi and his brothers continued to hover around Asher and Emily, as if ready to intervene if Emily needed it. It wasn't Asher's proudest moment. He went down on his knees beside Emily and gave her a tissue Kenzi had pushed into his hand. "Emily, I'll get a plane readied. We can be there in a couple hours."

Emily took a deep breath and pushed herself to her feet. She blew her nose in the tissue and reached for her phone. "I can't think. I need to get out of here." She dialed a number then said, "Celeste, I'm hiring a car to take me back to Welchton. My museum is burning down." She was quiet for a moment then said, "You don't have to. I know you have work. Okay, if you're sure." She hung up and wiped the tears from her eyes. "I'll send for my things later. I just need to grab my purse and call for a car."

Asher stood in front of her. "I'm going with you."

She shook her head. "No, you're not."

Kenzi stepped closer. "I can go with you, Emily."

Emily shook her head and tears spilled down her cheeks again. "This may be a horrible thing to say, but if any of you had anything to do with this, I could never forgive you. I could never even look at you again."

Emily rushed out of the room and up the stairs to get her purse, leaving Asher to face his siblings. "As far as I know, I didn't do this."

Kenzi made a sound of disgust. "As far as you know? How can you not know?"

Andrew came to stand beside Kenzi. "I see it even in the

Marines. When you instill the idea that winning at any cost is the goal, then there will always be those who will do anything not to fail."

Ian took his place beside Asher. "What are you going to do?"

Asher watched Emily rush down the stairs and out the front door of his parents' home. He could have, but he didn't chase her. "I'm going to find out who is responsible."

Ian asked, "What happens if you are?"

Asher shook his head. For the first time in his life he really had no idea what he would do. There was a good chance the blame lay at his door. He was angrier with himself than with anyone who stood in judgment of him.

Fuck.

Chapter Sixteen

EARLY THE NEXT morning Emily stood on the porch of the guest house and stared at what was left of her grandfather's house. No matter how long she looked at the charred remains and the safety tape the firefighters had encircled them with, she couldn't believe it.

Two firefighters and the fire marshal were still there, sifting through the debris for the cause of the fire. She'd been told she'd need to wait to approach the area herself; they would tell her if anything had survived the fire. It was easy to see that not much would have. The entire building had collapsed in on itself.

By the time Emily had arrived last night, firefighters were dousing certain areas with additional water, but most of the fire was out. They said it had been fully developed by the time they'd arrived on the scene.

She'd heard one of the firefighters say, "It's a shame the sprinkler system wasn't functioning. It might have saved the building."

Emily covered her face with her hands as she remembered the comment. She'd had the system installed and a preliminary inspection done, but it was turned off, pending one final modification. She'd been saving up the money to pay to have it completed. When she thought about the money she'd put into renovating the interior, she felt like crying again. *If I had finished the sprinkler system first and put the renovations off, I wouldn't have lost everything.*

A pain was ripping through her that sought someone or something to blame. Emily had spent half the night before hating herself and the other half hating Asher and his family.

The whole scenario was too convenient to not have been orchestrated. When she'd set off to Boston to threaten Asher, she'd never thought it could possibly come to this. He'd told her again and again that winning was what mattered to him and how he would go about it. *"When I want something, I assess what is standing between me and what I want, then I remove the obstacle."* He'd also said he didn't care about her land. Well, he'd certainly shown how much he meant that.

The pain of his betrayal cut so deeply it drained Emily of the anger from the night before and left her feeling hollow. *Was any of it real? Was I ever more than an obstacle to him?*

Emily felt a coat being wrapped around her shoulders and lowered her hands. Steam wafted upward from the cup of hot coffee Celeste held out to her. Emily accepted it automatically. "Thank you."

"How long have you been out here?" Celeste asked.

"I don't know."

"Your phone has been ringing all morning."

Emily put the cup down on the porch railing and re-turned her gaze to where the firefighters were working. "I don't care."

Celeste took a sip of her coffee. "Brrr. It's cold out here. Why don't we go inside?"

"I'm fine."

After a long moment, Celeste said, "This has to be hell for you, but there are things you need to do today. I contacted your insurance company. They're sending out an investigator. They're going to ask you some tough questions, Emily, and we might want to talk about what your answers should be."

"I don't have any answers. I don't have anything anymore."

Celeste placed her coffee beside Emily's and turned her friend to face her. "Stop it. You need to snap out of this. I called one of my friends who works in insurance, and she thinks a situation like this will spark a full investigation of everything from your finances to your association with the Barrington family. They'll be looking for fraud and the possibility of bringing criminal charges against someone. Is there anything I need to know?"

"I don't understand."

"Did you move money? Pay anyone in cash? Anything that would make you look guilty?"

"Guilty? How could you think I would burn my grandfather's house down?"

"It doesn't matter what I think, it matters how it will look to the investigator and, possibly, to the police. Let's face it—you're the last unsold house. Maybe you thought your museum was worth more than B&H was offering. Maybe you paid someone to burn it down so you could get the insurance money and then more money for your land."

"That's insane. My mother's artwork was in there."

"Some pieces, yes, but you moved most of them to Boston for the exhibit. Did you do that because you knew this place would burn?"

Emily searched her friend's face. "You know I'd never do that."

Celeste gave her a little shake. "Yes, I know that, but what are you going to say when the investigator asks you these questions? You have to be prepared."

"He's going to want to know why I took out more insurance." Emily closed her eyes and covered them with one hand.

"Holy shit, Em."

Emily opened her eyes and turned her gaze back to the remnants of her museum. "I have nothing to hide. I didn't do anything wrong. Grant Barrington is a financial wizard. He offered to help me organize my resources. He's the one who suggested I increase my coverage."

"Okay, that's good. When the investigator asks, have him speak to Grant."

"I can't. I told you I ran out of there last night, but I didn't tell you what I said to them before I left. I accused them of being responsible for this."

Celeste gasped. "I can't say the thought hasn't crossed my mind, but I don't know if I would have said it to them."

Without turning to her friend, Emily clenched her hands at her sides and asked, "You always say you have a better read of people than I do. Did they do this to me?"

Celeste cringed. "I don't know, Em. They seemed to genuinely like you. What did Asher say?"

"He said he doesn't condone arson, but he didn't say his company was innocent. I don't know if I would have believed him even if he had."

"I'm calling a lawyer for you. You need someone who knows what to do."

Emily shook her head sadly. "I know you're right, Celeste, and normally I'd be scared, but I'm numb—just numb. I feel like I've lost my family all over again."

Celeste put an arm around Emily and hugged her. "You have me, Em. You're not alone. We'll figure this out."

Emily wiped away her tears. She felt badly that Celeste was being pulled into her problems. Although Emily was grateful, all she really wanted to do was dig a hole somewhere and hide from the world. She forced a brave smile solely for the benefit of her friend. "Don't think you have to stay. I know this is a critical time for your agency."

Celeste pulled her coat tighter around her. "It is, but the perk of being the boss is I can take time off when I need to. If this happened to me, you'd be with me. I'm not going anywhere."

ASHER LOOSENED HIS tie, kicked off his shoes, and sank into the couch of his finally quiet office. Day two of hunting for answers and he didn't feel closer to the truth. He checked his phone, but neither his call nor his text to Emily had been answered. Not that he could blame her; even he was beginning to think he was to blame.

Over the past forty-eight hours, he'd held meeting after meeting and questioned countless employees on the side; what he'd discovered made him sick. His plow-through-any-obstacle philosophy didn't look as pretty on the front lines. His people were too smart to break the law, but they stretched it, used it to their advantage, and essentially forced people to accept an offer.

Would any of them have gone as far as arson?

His most trusted team was in Trundaie. His personal assistant, Ryan, had been helpful in organizing the interviews, but he'd looked nervous when Asher had questioned him about the museum. He'd admitted to receiving a threatening call from the construction company B&H had preliminarily contacted to build the new facility. Had the deal been finalized it would have been a financial windfall for them.

If they were responsible, Asher hadn't been able to find evidence of it.

Asher hadn't been back to his parents' house since the night Emily had left. He couldn't face his family anymore than he could face Emily. He needed to know if the fire was his fault, and if it was, he needed to make it right.

A New Hampshire news station had reported on the fire and the story had gone national. Emily's innocence or guilt was being debated at water coolers and on talk shows. Those who thought she was guilty cited desperation and greed as her motivation. Either way, the Welchton police had named Emily Harris as a person of interest, despite the initial report that stated an electrical fire as the cause.

Asher closed his eyes even though he knew he would never sleep. He wanted to call Celeste again, but he didn't. He'd spoken to her twice in the past two days. The first time had been all about getting Emily to speak to him and when that failed, finding out from Celeste about how Emily was doing. The second time he spoke to Celeste he convinced her to let him help Emily any way he could. He called in favors to make sure Emily was represented pro bono by the best lawyer in New England.

Emily might not want his protection, but she had it. He had people watching her home to make sure it wasn't vandalized and watching her to make sure she was safe. Media attention had a way of leading crazies to a person's door.

His phone rang. *Ian.* "What do you want?"

"Are you sleeping in your office again?"

"Does it matter?"

"We're all worried about you."

"That's not the impression I got the other night."

Ian made a frustrated sound. "Mom isn't handling this well. Emily refuses to take calls from any of us. Mom wants us to fly up there and—I don't actually know what we would do. Camp in her yard? Drag her back here? We closed Emily's exhibit. I'm trying to convince Mom to call off next week's auction. People are already pulling out, and it's only getting worse. Get your ass over here and help me with damage control."

Asher stood and went to look out his office window. "I

need to know if I'm responsible. If one of my people did this, I need to make it right. No matter what happens to me."

"You need to be really careful with this situation. It has national attention. You could put our family and your company in jeopardy."

Asher punched the wall beside him with the side of his fist. "I love her, Ian. It took me long enough to realize it, but I did. I don't want to be the reason she lost her museum. I want to be the man she hoped I was."

Asher thought of his father and the scandal that had ended his career. He finally understood the choice his father had made; he understood there had been no choice at all. Nothing mattered more to his father than his mother's happiness, just as nothing mattered more to Asher than Emily's. How much would he risk for her? Everything if he had to.

"Have you found evidence proving it wasn't an electrical fire?"

"No."

"Then it was probably just a spark. No one's fault."

"I can't sleep, Ian. I can't eat. I need to know the truth."

"Whatever you discover, Asher, you can always come home. That's the beauty of home. Family takes you in when everyone else wants to string you up."

His brother's joke brought a curl to Asher's lips. "At least I know you'll visit me in prison."

"Even if it was arson, you didn't order it. What would they convict you of?"

"Murder," Asher said coldly. "Because if someone did

this to Emily I will kill them with my bare hands."

"Okay, well, that is probably all we should say over the phone. I'll come see you tomorrow. Try to get some rest."

After they hung up, Asher dropped the phone into his trouser pocket and continued to look over the dark city. He'd worked insane hours for as long as he could remember to make B&H the success it was. It was all that had mattered. If he was guilty and went public with it, he would be risking it all to save Emily.

It wasn't something he needed to think twice about. As soon as he had his answers he would go to her and do whatever needed to be done to make it right.

A throat cleared, and Asher spun on his heel at the sound. A beautiful redhead in a silk business suit was seated at his desk. "Who the hell are you, and what are you doing here?"

She took out a black card with white print and pushed it across his desk toward him. Asher picked the card up. All it had on it was a phone number. "Dominic Corisi sent me."

Asher threw the card down and barked, "Tell him I have too much on my plate right now to get involved in anything else."

The woman tapped her polished nails on the top of his desk. "Didn't your mother teach you to never turn down an offer until you know what it is?"

"I'm not interested. Now get out."

The woman crossed her legs and gave him a head-to-toe assessment. "I wouldn't throw me out yet. The AFT is still investigating your girlfriend. You're not any closer to finding

ALWAYS MINE

out if the fire in Welchton was arson, and I'm probably your only hope if you want the truth. That is what you want, isn't it? To know what really happened?"

Asher put two hands on his desk and growled, "Do you have information about the fire?"

The redhead stood. "I have information about everything, and what I don't know, I can find out in twenty-four hours. But before I look into this for you, I need to ask you something. Do you really want the truth? It may not be what you want to hear."

"Of course I want the fucking truth, but how do I know if I should believe anything you say?"

The woman smiled. "Call Dominic. He sent me. I'm the person he goes to when he needs information. You don't need my name, but you should keep my card." She walked around the desk and paused by a package Asher had forgotten was still on one of his shelves. She traced the return address with one of her nails. "And if you really are seeking the truth, you'll want to read this."

Asher frowned. "That's a gift from my cousins. It wouldn't have anything to do with the fire."

"I never said it would." The woman walked to the door. "You'll have a flash drive on your desk tomorrow evening. The password will be the name of your second grade teacher. Dominic doesn't ask me to look after very many people, so you should consider yourself lucky."

Asher followed the woman out the door of his office and past Ryan's desk. Both should have been high-security areas. "Hey, how did you get past my security?"

She rolled her eyes skyward and said, "Call the number on the card. Ask for Marc Stone. He'll have a report and some suggestions for you." Then she walked out of Ryan's office. Asher called downstairs and told his security officers to make sure she left the building. They weren't happy someone had gotten by them.

He called Dominic and asked him if he'd sent anyone over to see him. Dominic confirmed that he had, but he also gave him a warning similar to the one the redhead had. "There's always a risk when using Alethea."

"What kind of risk?"

"She's too good at what she does. Once she starts digging she can't stop. You will never have a secret again. But she'll get the truth for you."

Asher slept fitfully on the couch in his office. When he woke, he went back to his apartment to shower and change. He spent the day interviewing more of his employees, but no one, not even Hearne was cracking. When he returned to his office there was a flash drive on his desk just as the woman had said there would be.

Out of caution, he pulled a laptop out of a cabinet. He knew enough about computer viruses to not expose his server with whatever was on the flash drive. While he waited for the laptop to download, he poured himself a shot of whiskey. Whatever the truth was, Emily and her safety were what mattered.

Chapter Seventeen

"COME TO BOSTON with me," Celeste said between bites of pizza.

Emily took one bite then placed her slice back on her paper plate. "You heard the insurance adjuster. He said I shouldn't leave until the investigation is complete."

Celeste stood, walked to the refrigerator in the guest house, and took out a bottled water. "Want one?" Emily shook her head, but Celeste placed one in front of her anyway. "Your lawyer said you could go anywhere you want to. The official investigation is complete. What they're doing now is a witch-hunt. They don't want to pay you, and they're trying to find a reason not to."

Emily pushed her plate away. "I don't even care about the money."

Celeste took a swig of her water and said, "Great, then give it to me. Along with all of your mother's paintings and your sculptures. Due to all the exposure on the news, your artwork is probably worth more now. Maybe I'll take that trip to Hawaii I've been putting off. Or buy a bigger condo."

Emily glared at Celeste. "That's not funny."

Celeste stood up. "No, it's not, but I'm sick of this pity party. You can't stay here, stare at the past all day long, and convince yourself you're going to lose your mind. You know what, this sucks. You're right. You lost something you loved, but it was a building, Em. It was wood and plaster and wires that rodents apparently found delicious. You can't spend the rest of your life mourning it."

Emily stood and threw her hands up in the air. "It was more than a building. It was my dream."

"It was your mother's dream, and you wanted to make it a reality. Open your eyes. The building burning was probably the best thing that could have happened. The town you remember is gone. You were holding on to a dream that couldn't have happened here anyway. You are an amazing person, Em, and I love you, but I can't fight this battle for you. I can't make you want to stand up and try again." Celeste's eyes filled with tears and her voice cracked. "And it scares me because I can't stay, but I can't leave you here, either. So, what are we going to do?"

Emily walked over and hugged her friend. Seeing herself through her friend's eyes was not easy, but there was comfort in the numbness that had shrouded her since the fire. Starting over would mean facing not only what had happened to her, but what she had done and how she felt. Celeste had left Welchton and had made a new life for herself. *I can be brave like that. I can pick myself up and start over.* "Celeste, I blamed Asher and his family. I said awful things to them. How do I face any of them again?"

Celeste hugged her tightly. "What would you tell me to

do if I were you?"

Emily walked over and took a long drink of water before answering. "I'd tell you to suck it up, get your ass back to Boston, and say whatever you need to say to get your collection back. Then I'd remind you that a museum is about the work inside it, not the location of it."

Celeste raised her water bottle in a toast. "That's the Emily I know."

The water bottle in Emily's hand was shaking so much she put it down. "I have to go back."

"Yes, you do."

"I really believed the Barringtons were guilty. And Asher. What does it say about me that I slept with a man I thought was capable of this?"

Celeste made a face. "I am not for Asher or against him. I believe he cares about you, but a relationship takes two, Em. I've known you a long time. You're not paranoid. If you doubted him, he gave you reason to."

Emily thought about how he'd left her in Paris and all the things he'd said that had made a damning argument against him when her trust had been tested. She missed him, but she didn't see a way back to him. "I don't even know what I would say if I saw him again."

"Give yourself time. You'll figure it out. Until then, what do you want to do?"

Emily squared her shoulders. "My lawyer said he could get me a draw check, something to tide me over until the insurance company settles the claim. What do you think about me putting my stuff in storage and traveling a little bit? Maybe you're right; this isn't where I belong anymore."

"You don't have to decide today."

"I don't want to be this sad any longer, Celeste. There's nothing here for me anymore. You saw the truth, but I didn't want to. I can't rebuild. What would be the point? Who wants to drive an hour through a ghost town to visit a museum filled with artwork from two unknown artists?"

"If you start whining again I will pour this water over your head."

Emily held up a hand in mock defense. "No need. I'm not complaining; I'm assessing the obstacles in my way. The Harris Tactile Museum will happen, but not here." She rubbed a hand across her forehead. "I wonder if B&H still wants the land. I'll have my lawyer look into it."

Celeste's jaw dropped open. "You'd sell it to them? What about the guest house?"

"My grandfather built it for his wife, and he's with her now. He wouldn't want it to hold me back. If I sell, I can use the money to buy a new place or rent somewhere." Emily walked over to the window and looked out at the blackened remains. "This dream didn't happen, but it can make the next one possible. My mother would approve. She was not a quitter."

And neither am I. Neither am I.

THE NEXT DAY, Asher stood behind his office desk and stretched. It had been one hell of a week, but he'd made progress in the areas he'd needed to. Thanks to Alethea, Asher had evidence that the cause of the fire was a wire that had been chewed through by a rodent who had built a nest inside one of the walls. He also had a photo of the insurance investigator kissing a woman who was not his wife. That photo had been in a file labeled "additional motivational material if necessary." Blackmail hadn't been necessary; Asher's lawyers had taken the evidence the fire marshal had submitted and brought it to the attention of the insurance company again. In case they had missed it.

With that done, Asher was free to turn his attention back to the more complicated issue of getting Emily to speak to him again. He'd received an email from her lawyer that she wanted to sell to B&H. He'd immediately tried to call her, but his call went to voice mail. He considered flying there and forcing her to see him, but he'd spent a lot of time thinking about why she'd believed the worst of him.

Because I've shown my worst to her.

He wanted to earn her trust this time. His father had told him she didn't need a hammer, and he'd been right. Emily had dreams of her own and deserved to be with a man who supported them. He'd never imagined himself with a wife or family, but the idea of never waking beside Emily again was unacceptable.

Dominic had moved from the world Asher was in to a place he said allowed him to look himself in the mirror each day. Seeing him in action inspired Asher to reevaluate his plan for what came after Trundaie. He'd bring Bennett Stone stateside and do a better job of patrolling how B&H's policies were implemented. He hadn't been guilty of Emily's fire, but he could have been, and that wasn't what he wanted for himself or his company.

Ryan beeped in via the intercom. "Your uncles are here."

"Who?"

"Alessandro and Victor Andrade. They said they have an appointment."

"Send them in."

Two older Italian men entered. One with a big smile, one with a more reserved expression. Asher knew them only from photos, old photos his mother took out around the holidays. Asher closed the door in the face of a curious Ryan. "Gentlemen, have a seat."

"Thank you," they said in unison and sat down.

Asher leaned back against the front of his desk. "You do realize we're not related."

Alessandro said, "Your mother's sister married our oldest brother."

Asher nodded. "Exactly."

Victor said, "By my definition, that's family."

Asher folded his arms across his chest. "We'll have to agree to disagree on that point."

"Victor, doesn't he remind you of Gio?"

"Gio? No. He's Max. Look at the nose."

Asher raised a hand. "Was there something you wanted?"

Alessandro waved his hands as he spoke. "Your brother Lance has come to some of our family's events, but not you. How can we change that?"

Asher rubbed his hands over his face. He was tired, hungry, and desperately missing Emily. He wasn't in the mood to pander to self-labeled family, not while he was still smoothing things over with his real one. "I wish I had more time, but I have somewhere I need to be." *It's called anywhere but here.*

Victor looked around the office before meeting Asher's gaze. "The older Alessandro and I get, the more sentimental we become. To an Andrade, family is everything."

Asher straightened. "I'm a Barrington."

Alessandro smiled. "You're right, Victor. He has a lot of Max in him."

Victor leaned forward. "Family isn't defined by blood alone. I sent Dominic to see you because he understands that. And I don't want to push, but a little gratitude would be appropriate."

Instead of thanking him, Asher asked, "Why the hell do you care what happens to me? You didn't care about my father."

Alessandro stood and turned to Victor. "What is he talking about?"

Victor shrugged. "I bet it's the scandal." He turned back to Asher. "Dale asked us to stay out of it. We offered to help him."

Asher shook his head slowly. "Why would my father turn down help from *family?*" He spoke the last word with thick sarcasm.

Victor and Alessandro exchanged a look, then Victor said, "Your Aunt Patrice was not the nicest woman, but your mother loved her. At the time, there were rumors that Patrice was jealous of your mother's happiness and tried to ruin it. Your mother didn't believe she was capable of that kind of vindictiveness. She begged your father not to go up against her sister. Your father had to choose between his wife's happiness and his reputation. You saw the result. He lost his political career, but he and your mother are still together, no?"

Asher's head was spinning. "Why are you telling me this?"

"Two reasons," Alessandro said.

Victor continued, "One, we are so upset over what we're hearing about your mother's auction. What is wrong with the people here? They can't see that your girlfriend's innocent? A little hint of fraud sends them all scurrying away? We can't sit back and watch Sophie be humiliated over this. We want to come to the auction."

"I'll talk to my mother," Asher said and looked at the door in a not-so-subtle hint for them to leave.

"Tell her we will bid fifty . . . a hundred . . . maybe two hundred. Just to be safe."

"I'll have her call you," Asher promised and started toward the door.

"Wait," Alessandro said. "There is the other matter."

Asher froze and turned on his heel.

Victor went to stand beside Alessandro. "Are you in love with Emily Harris?"

Asher turned back and strode to the door. "I'm not doing this." He started to open the door.

Both Alessandro and Victor sat back down. Alessandro said, "Victor, he doesn't think he needs us."

Victor arched an eyebrow. "I bet she's not even talking to

him."

"Get the fuck out of my office," Asher growled.

"He's rude," Victor said dryly.

"And he still hasn't said thank you."

Asher's temper rose. "I don't want to manhandle two old men, but you need to leave."

"He called you old," Alessandro said with a chuckle.

"You, too," Victor said and shrugged.

"Did you ever think we'd be the matchmakers of the family?"

"No, but this one desperately needs our help."

Am I sleeping? Because this is a nightmare. "What do I need to do to get you out of my office?"

Alessandro looked over his shoulder at Asher. "We are both happily married and, not to toot our own horns, but we're very good in the romance department, if you know what I mean."

"I really don't want to know."

Victor asked, "Do you want to marry Emily Harris, or not?"

Asher groaned then said, "Yes."

Alessandro slapped a hand on the edge of Asher's desk. "Then sit down, son, because you've got a lot to learn about women."

Chapter Eighteen

E MILY STUFFED HER cold hands into the pockets of her jacket and walked up the steps of the Barrington home. The front door opened before Emily had time to ring the bell.

"It's good see you, Emily," Dale said and stepped back. "Come in." He closed the door then asked if he could take her coat.

Emily shook her head. She was cold to the bone and shaking. Not too many things intimidated her, but the Barringtons had been kind to her, and she had repaid them by accusing them of arson. She wouldn't blame them if they didn't accept her apology and threw her out. There was no way around seeing them again, though. Partly because she needed to get her collection back and partly because she felt badly about everything she'd said the night of the fire. "How is Sophie?"

He stared at her without answering, then finally said, "It was a difficult week for her. It always is, but she was upset that you thought any of us would ever hurt you."

Emily hugged her coat closer. "I was wrong, and I'm here

to apologize."

"And to get your artwork, I would imagine."

Emily swallowed hard. "Yes, that too."

"Have you spoken to Asher?"

Emily looked away and blinked back tears. "No. What could I say? I really thought he had done it. I can't imagine he could forgive me for that."

Dale's face was carefully devoid of expression. He was looking at her as if she were a stranger. *And why wouldn't he? After everything I said?* "Come with me to the solarium. Sophie is looking forward to seeing you."

Sophie put down the book she was reading and stood as soon as she heard them enter. She crossed the room and hugged Emily.

That was all it took for Emily to burst into tears. She cried for several minutes in Sophie's arms as the woman murmured to her as mothers do. She cried because she missed her mother and felt she was letting her go all over again. She cried because she knew she had hurt Sophie, and the woman had done so much for her. To round it off, she sobbed because Emily knew when she'd lost Asher, she'd lost his family, too.

Sophie put a tissue in her hand and led her to the settee. "Oh, Emily. Everything is going to be okay."

Emily blew her nose, roughly wiped her tears away, and gave herself a mental shake. "I didn't come here to cry all over you. I wanted you know how badly I feel about what I said to you. What I said to all of you. You were so good to me, and I hurt you. I'm so sorry I didn't answer your calls. I didn't know what to say."

Sophie looked over Emily's head and said, "Dale, could you have the cook bring us some sandwiches and tea? Emily looks like she hasn't eaten in a week." She brought her gaze back to Emily and gave her a pat on the knee. "Oh, Emily, sweetie, you were in shock. You didn't know what you were saying. Let's put all that behind us."

Emily almost burst into tears again. *I needed to hear that, Sophie. You have no idea how much I needed that. I never wanted to disappoint you.* Aloud she said, "Thank you, Sophie. You have no idea how much that means to me."

After a quiet moment in which Sophie blinked back her own tears, she said, "The news said the fire was electrical and caused by rodents?"

"Yes. It was in the part of the house I hadn't renovated yet."

"I've no doubt you must have been devastated. Still are. That house meant so much to you, let alone the museum. How long will it take you to rebuild?"

"I sold my land to B&H. I won't be rebuilding."

Sophie's lips rounded in surprise, but whatever she would have said was cut short by the appearance of Dale. A member of their house staff placed tea and a tray of sandwiches on a table beside Sophie. Sophie waited until the staff had stepped away before she said, "Asher bought her property."

Dale didn't say anything, but his lips pressed together in displeasure.

Emily hastened to add, "The idea to sell was mine. I'm

going to use the money to start over somewhere else. Artwork is meant to be seen, and it wouldn't have been seen in Welchton. Now I'm free to find the best place for my museum . . . and for me."

Sophie poured Emily a cup of tea and handed it to her. "Your exhibit is still intact if you would like to reopen before the auction. You are still participating in the auction, aren't you?"

Dale stood behind Sophie and placed a hand on her shoulder as they both waited for Emily's response. Although Emily had come with the intention of apologizing and then organizing how to move her things to storage, she found herself saying, "If you still want me to."

Sophie smiled at Dale, who nodded with approval. "I'll leave you two ladies to talk. I have a few calls to make."

Once they were alone again, Emily said, "The news reporters made a huge deal out of the investigation that followed the fire. I wasn't sure you'd want that kind of publicity associated with your event."

Sophie poured herself a cup of tea and shook her head sadly. "There are some who won't come, but they'll wish they had when they see how well we do without them."

Emily smiled for the first time that day. Sophie reminded her of her own mother at times—strong in ways that mattered. "The worst of it should be over now. The insurance company closed the investigation and accepted the fire marshal's findings."

"You must be relieved."

Emily shrugged. "I was in shock through most of it. It's

all sort of a blur."

"Was Celeste with you?"

Emily put her tea down and picked up a sandwich. "She stayed until last night. We drove back to Boston together."

"I like her," Sophie said.

"Me, too. She's a good friend."

After a quiet moment, Sophie said, "Emily, we have all missed you and are very sorry for your loss. The others are coming to dinner tonight. Can you stay so they can see you too?"

The idea of seeing Asher's brothers and sister made her hands cold and clammy again. Would they be as quick to accept her apology as Sophie? Would Emily have been if the situation were reversed? "I'll see them at the auction."

Sophie sipped her tea. "Have you seen Asher yet?"

Emily dropped her sandwich to the floor, picked it up, brushed it off, then didn't know what else to do with it so she put it back on her plate. "Not yet."

"He looks as exhausted as you do. He was afraid he might have been responsible."

Emily blinked a few times at the confirmation that she looked as bad as she thought, then focused on the more important part of what she'd said. "He wasn't, though."

"No, but he could have been, and we all know it. I felt awful about what I said to him the night of the fire, but he needed to hear it. This week has been good for him. He needed to wake up and see where he was headed."

Emily hesitated before sharing more with Sophie, but she craved some maternal advice. "He has been calling me, but I haven't answered him. I was angry with him at first, and then I was sad. Now all I can think is that too much has happened, and if I were him I wouldn't forgive me."

Sophie put down her cup and laid her hand on Emily's arm. "I grew up thinking I had to be perfect. My father was a very wealthy man, and he wanted the best of everything. The best house, the most beautiful wife, and daughters who were perfectly groomed to marry the men he chose for us. My sister was the first to defy him. She married an Italian straight from Italy. It was so romantic and that gave me the courage to choose Dale. My father was furious with both of us. I moved north to live with Dale, and I don't regret that choice even though it meant I wasn't there when my mother passed away. Patrice and her husband stayed with our father. She wasn't happy, and she blamed me for some of that. I had to cut them out of my life because they couldn't love me, not the way a father should love his daughter or a woman should love her sister. Was the rift my fault? I don't know. Maybe I could have tried harder to make amends with them. I'm not perfect, Emily. My children certainly aren't, either. You don't have to be perfect to be part of this family, you just have to love my son."

"I do," Emily whispered.

"I hope I'm not interrupting," Kenzi said as she walked into the room. "I heard Emily was here." She took a seat across from them.

Emily leaned forward and said, "Kenzi, I can't begin to tell you—"

"Mom, I had the most interesting conversation with

Asher this morning." Kenzi wasn't looking at Emily, and she felt she might cry again. She had thought she and Kenzi would become friends, but it now didn't seem likely.

"Asher?" Emily blurted then regained control and told herself to not intrude in their family's business.

"He asked for my help with something. Imagine that. Asher asked me for help."

Sophie's voice rose with her curiosity. "What does he want you to do?"

"He asked me not to say," Kenzi said. The expression on her face implied she'd considered refusing his request. Her gaze returned to Emily. "Does he know you're back in Boston?" Her tone was cooler than Emily was used to hearing from her. Emily couldn't blame her, but it hurt to think what she'd said might have destroyed their friendship.

"I haven't spoken to him."

Kenzi shrugged. "Dad called me. He may have told him." Emily's attention flew to the door of the solarium, them back to Kenzi. "You think he might be on his way?"

"I don't know."

Emily stood. She wanted to see Asher again, but not like this, not with an audience. The last thing she wanted to do was start crying again in front of Sophie. "I can't . . . I have to go." The sound of the front door opening and closing had Emily scrambling for her purse. "Sophie, I'll call you about the auction."

Andrew and Lance strolled into the room and smiled when they saw Emily. Lance said, "Dad said Emily was here."

Andrew winked at Emily. "We figured we would all celebrate her not going to jail and Asher not being the ass who sent her there."

"Andrew," Sophie admonished and shook her head at the joke.

"Too soon?" Andrew asked. His smile was irresistible.

Emily wasn't upset. She and Andrew had thrown several jokes back and forth in the short time they'd known each other. "What do you call a Marine with an IQ of 150?"

Andrew's eyes narrowed, but he was smiling in anticipation of the punch line.

"A platoon," Emily said with a huge smile.

Lance laughed. "Ouch, she got you."

Andrew joined in the laughter then waved a finger at Emily. "Oh, just wait. I will find the perfect artist joke."

Grant stepped into the room and said, "All that laughing can only mean one thing. Emily, are you staying for dinner?"

Emily met his eyes hesitantly. Of all of Asher's siblings, he had put aside the most time to help her design a financial plan for the museum. "Grant, I am so sorry about what I said."

Grant shrugged a shoulder. "That was a horrific night for you. I'm sure we can all put it behind us."

Ian appeared at Grant's side. "Dad called and told me to get my ass over here, but I was at B&H because Asher wanted to talk to me about something. What did I miss?"

Kenzi cocked her head to one side. "Wait, Asher asked you for help too? Did he swear you to secrecy?"

"Maybe," Ian answered vaguely.

"Me, too," Andrew and Lance said at the same time.

Grant looked skyward and said, "And here I was thinking I was the special one."

Sophie looked around at each of her children and said, "What is going on?"

That's exactly what I'm asking myself, Emily thought, but before anyone answered, Dale came back into the room. He said a few words to each of his children then looked at Emily. "Can I speak to you for a moment? Alone?"

Emily's stomach clenched nervously. "Sure." They stepped off to one side of the room and Emily held her breath while she waited. He couldn't be upset with her, could he? If he was, why would he have called all of his children to come home while she was there?

"You and Asher have some things you need to figure out before we can have you stay here again." His tone was firmer than Emily was used to hearing from him.

It wasn't what Emily had expected to hear, but she held her tears back and told herself he was only saying what she knew was true. If things didn't work out with Asher, she didn't belong there. "I understand."

Looking into Dale's eyes, Emily saw why Sophie had defied her father for him. He was a kind man even when he was protecting his family. "But I want you to know that we care about you."

Emily blinked, but she couldn't hold back the tears. She wiped them away as quickly as they fell. "Thank you, Dale."

"Don't you cry, or I'll get a lecture from Sophie."

Emily sniffed and smiled. "I blubbered all over her, I'm

sure she won't blame you. Believe it or not, I'm not usually so emotional."

"I hope you're around long enough to back up that claim."

Emily nodded, although she wasn't at all sure she would be. "Did you call Asher?"

"No. You two need to figure this out on your own."

He makes it sound so easy. "Do you want me to go now? I feel strange leaving after everyone just got here."

He gave her a sympathetic look. "Stay for a while, Emily, but perhaps not for dinner. I'd love to see you marry into the family. I just don't know if my son can pull his head out of his ass long enough to make that happen."

IN ADDITION TO his regular work, Asher spent the day preparing before he went to see Emily. He wasn't going to plow forward with Emily. He had a plan.

He hated to admit it, but Alessandro and Victor made a solid argument, modifying his methods. If anyone would have told him he'd be taking relationship advice from two old men, Asher would have laughed the idea off, but the longer they'd spoken, the more what they'd said made sense.

According to Alessandro there were four steps to winning a woman's heart.

"Step One: The Grand Gesture. Women say all they need is for you to love them, but they actually need more than that. They need tangible evidence that the man they are about to spend the rest of their lives with is willing to move heaven and earth for them.

"Step Two: The Talk. Address the problem. Don't make excuses. And it's not enough to say you're sorry, you have to know why. Women ask a lot of questions. Some can be tricky to navigate. Prepare responses ahead of time.

"Step Three: The Proclamation. If it's love, say it. A proposal, do it. Don't leave much time between the talk and the proclamation or Step One will be necessary again.

"Step Four: The Sex."

Asher had stopped Alessandro there and thought about Emily's offer to sell her land. He completed his personal purchase of the rest of the property in that town and had told the lawyer to move forward with purchasing hers.

Grand Gesture? I'll show those two geezers a grand gesture. He'd met with each of his siblings and had given them tasks to help make it happen, then had sworn them to secrecy.

He wasn't overly worried about Step Two. She was the one who had accused him wrongly, but he'd prepared a brief apology anyway. If two simple words were what was standing between him and waking up next to her every morning, he'd say them gladly.

Step Three required some reflection and then a trip into the city to buy the perfect diamond. If time had allowed, he would have designed her ring, but he wasn't waiting past the night of the auction to propose.

He'd cleared his schedule for work the day after the auction in anticipation of Step Four.

All in all, Asher was feeling confident that everything would go smoothly. All he had to do now was convince Emily to come back to Boston for the auction.

Ryan beeped in. "There's a woman here to see you."

Asher checked the time on his watch. It was almost six. "Tell her I'm busy."

"It's Ms. Harris."

Asher stood up with a force that sent his chair flying into the wall behind his desk. "Send her in."

Emily stepped into his office, looking so beautifully fragile Asher wanted to rush to her side, pull her into his arms, and kiss her, but he didn't. He'd said he wouldn't plow over her feelings, and he was determined not to.

"Can we talk?" she asked.

Shit. Talking was supposed to come after the Grand Gesture. He walked around his desk and motioned to a chair. "Have a seat."

"I'd rather stand."

The conversation reminded him of the first time he'd met her. In retrospect, he admired the courage she'd shown by coming to Boston to tell him to his face what she thought of his offer. Had she not done that, they wouldn't have met. Asher didn't want to say or do anything that would make her walk out of his life again. He didn't know if he should say he was sorry she'd lost her museum or let her bring it up.

She raised her chin and met his eyes. "I misjudged you, and I'm sorry. I should have trusted you."

Asher clenched his fists and took Alessandro's advice to choose his words carefully. "I gave you enough reasons not to."

Her eyebrows rose and lowered in agreement. "Still, I hope you'll accept my apology."

He stepped closer to her. He didn't want her to be sorry. He wanted to tell her all the ways he would be a better man for her. "Emily."

She put up a hand. "You were right about a lot of things. There was nothing left for me in New Hampshire. Even if it had all worked out the way I'd planned, it wouldn't have been what my mother and I had envisioned."

Asher didn't want to agree or disagree. "I'm sorry," he blurted out.

Emily's eyes filled with tears. "I'm sorry, too, but I don't know where we go from here. I want to believe we could get past this, but we keep coming right back to this place. How do I know we won't be here a month from now? How do I know . . .?"

That I would move heaven and earth for you?

He approached her. "Are you attending the auction?"

Emily nodded.

"Then I'll see you there."

Emily frowned, searched his face, and nodded. "Of course." She turned quickly away and started toward the door.

"Emily," Asher said as she opened the door.

"Yes?" she questioned, without turning around.

"The auction is an important night for all of us. Make sure you come."

She stood absolutely still for a moment, then said, "Your family has been very kind to me. I'll be there."

Chapter Nineteen

THE DAY OF the auction Emily met her eyes in the full-length mirror in the bathroom of Celeste's apartment. *I can do this.* She hadn't heard from Asher since she'd left his office, and she told herself it was for the best.

Seeing him had been torture. How could he dismiss her that way? Had he already moved on? *Women usually want to sleep with me, and it's never been more complicated than fitting them into my schedule. Well, he's always been honest, I have to give him that.*

How had he asked her to stay? *The auction is an important night for all of us.* That was probably the cue to remind her that she has no place in his family. In his life.

It was never supposed to be forever.

Celeste had said she'd encouraged Emily to go to Paris with Asher to wake her up, get her to see there was a whole world outside of Welchton. *I wasn't supposed to fall in love.*

She skimmed her profile in the mirror dispassionately. The dress was beautifully cut and clung to her curves. Celeste had organized hair and makeup to be done professionally, and the result was a polished look Emily's artistic eye appreciated, but she didn't feel beautiful. She felt confused.

If he cared about me, he would have tried to convince me to stay instead of agreeing with me that we could never work out.

After she'd walked out of Asher's office, she'd wanted to run back in and tell him she was being a fool and that, of course, she would try again. But she'd forced herself to keep walking.

I want the kind of love my grandfather had for my grandmother.

Did you feel like this when my father left you, Mom? How long does it hurt this badly?

Emily remembered asking her mother if she ever wished she'd never met her father. Her mother had said, "How could I ever regret anything that made you? Life is full of miracles and tragedies. We decide which is which and who we become because of them."

Mom, I'm trying to see the miracle in all of this. I wish you were here. I've always known where I was going and what I was doing. I don't know anything beyond my decision to finally give up.

Celeste snapped her fingers beside Emily. "The car is downstairs. Are you ready to go?"

She forced a smile to her lips. "I didn't get this gorgeous for nothing."

Celeste laughed. "That's the spirit. Let's go see how the one percent parties."

Emily turned away from the mirror. "I shouldn't drink tonight."

Celeste walked with her out of the bathroom and

through the bedroom. "I'm with you on that. Are you going to be okay if Asher is there?"

Emily wrapped a shawl around her shoulders. "I'll have to be, right? It'll be fine. We didn't end badly. We simply agreed not to try again."

Celeste grabbed a handful of tissues and stuffed them in her clutch bag. "Just in case."

"I'm fine," Emily protested. They walked out of the apartment to the elevator.

"I didn't say you weren't. It's been a long week for me, too. Give me a glass of wine and I might start bawling." She winked at Emily. "Especially if all the rich men there are married."

Emily slid into the back of a town car beside Emily. "What do you think tonight will be like?"

"Hard to say. Sophie's charity auctions are usually well attended and at the top of everyone's social calendar. It might not be like that this year."

Emily clutched her purse to her lap. "Because of me?"

"Do you want me to lie or can you handle the truth?"

"Lie."

"It has nothing to do with you."

No wonder Asher agreed to end our relationship. "I hope there's a good turnout, for Sophie's sake."

"Me, too."

They drove the rest of the way in tense silence. Celeste seemed to understand that Emily was too nervous to make light chitchat. There was a long line of cars in front of the auction building. "This is a good sign, right?" Emily asked.

"Absolutely," Celeste said in a positive tone. "Put on your brightest smile because it looks like the press is taking pictures as we go in."

ASHER SAW EMILY the moment she entered the building, but he didn't make a move to meet her. He had never seen her look more beautiful, but he had a feeling he would spend the rest of his life thinking that, each time he saw her. It took everything he had not to go to her, but he had a plan, and he was sticking to it. The crowd that filled the large bidding room spilled out into the surrounding rooms. Some of his mother's usual crowd was there. Those who had decided not to attend would regret their decision when the papers reported on those who had. Alessandro and Victor had not only invited their family, their enormous family, but had also invited their friends.

Brice Henderson came to stand beside him. "I didn't realize you knew half of these people."

"I don't," Asher said. He looked across the room to where Dominic and his wife were standing with Alessandro, Victor, and their wives. Alessandro noticed his attention was on them and raised a glass in salute. "But I have family who does."

"Are you sick?" Brice asked.

"No."

"Because you look like shit."

"Thanks. I haven't been sleeping well."

"Is it Trundaie? You said we had that under control."

"We do."

"Is it the New England site? Didn't you sort that out?"

"I did."

"I'm on schedule with the compound we need for Trundaie."

"Good."

"So, what the fuck is the problem?"

Asher took a deep breath and found Emily again in the crowd. "I'm going to ask Emily to marry me tonight."

"Here?"

"Yes."

"No wonder you look like you're about to have a stroke." He looked around the room as if searching for someone, then said, "Hey, is that James West? He's been trying to contact me, but I haven't had time to talk to him yet. What do you think he wants?"

Asher pulled his gaze away from Emily long enough to confirm the son of one of the largest oil refinery companies in the US was indeed in attendance. "I have no idea, but I've been meaning to talk to you about something, Brice. After Trundaie, I'll be making some changes in our policies and being more selective about which countries we partner with."

"Thank God."

Kenzi came to stand beside Asher. "Everything is set up. Emily's donation is scheduled as the last item. When it is brought out, a screen will come down behind the podium and out here in the hall. That's your cue to walk up to the podium."

Asher studied Kenzi's face, noting the line of concern on her forehead. "I love her, Kenzi."

Brice said, "That's my cue," and quickly stepped away.

Kenzi's gaze went from Asher to Emily and back. "I know, and I can see why. She's wonderful. I just don't want you to get hurt again."

A smile spread across Asher's face as he realized something. "You're worried about me."

Kenzi met his eyes. "You're my brother. Of course I'm worried about you."

Asher put his arm around Kenzi, pulled her to his side, and gave her a kiss on the top of the head. "I love you, too."

Kenzi pulled back and peered up at Asher. "Whoa. Did you just say what I think you said? I'm marking this date down on the calendar."

Asher sought out Emily again. She was beside Celeste, speaking to a senator. "You can, but it won't be the last time I say it. I took having a family for granted, but I won't anymore. I know that not everyone is as lucky as we are."

"You keep talking like that, and I'll have to forgive Emily."

Kenzi's love for Asher rocked him back on his heels. He took his family and their support for granted, but he wouldn't anymore. Kenzi wanted to protect him from getting hurt again, but she also needed to move past her anger. "You need to, Kenzi, because she's not going anywhere."

Chapter Twenty

A S THE AUCTION neared its conclusion, Emily told Celeste she had to go to the bathroom, and slipped out of the main room and into the hall. Her heart was pounding wildly in her chest and her palms were sweaty. She didn't need the bathroom; she was preparing to bolt.

Being in the same room as Asher and knowing it was over between them was a torture she couldn't endure one moment more. She knew she should stay and be there while her sculpture was auctioned off, but she couldn't do it. When the auction concluded, there wouldn't be another reason for her to see Asher. It would truly be over. She headed for the main exit and her escape.

"Emily," Ian stepped into her path, "have you met the Corisis? They were asking about you."

"No," Emily said. She looked behind her, then at the exit. "I'm sure I'll meet them afterward."

Lance walked up beside Ian. "Emily, I have a question about your sculpture. Do you mind walking over to see it with me? It'll just take a minute."

Emily sidestepped both of them. *I need a clean break. I'll hire someone to repack my collection, but I can't do this right now. I can't pretend this isn't killing me.* "Sorry, I was headed for the bathroom. Could we talk later?"

Grant stepped in front of her. "There is a bathroom inside."

She stepped around him too, beginning to feel trapped and frantic. "There was a long . . . I can't stay."

Andrew physically blocked her exit. "We have our orders. You are not to leave the building."

Emily looked from brother to brother. "What do you mean? Who told you I couldn't leave?"

Andrew looked to Grant. "Should we tell her or tackle her if she tries to make it past us?"

Shaking his head, Dale joined them. "If Emily wants to leave, let her go."

Lance waved a hand. "But Asher—"

"Why would Asher ask you to keep me here?" Emily searched all of their faces again.

Dale nodded toward the auction hall. "The only way to find out is to stay."

Emily looked across the room and saw Asher near the back of the room. He was watching her, but she couldn't read his expression. Were they all trying to make sure she didn't embarrass their mother by leaving early? "I don't understand."

Dale motioned for his sons to give him a moment to talk to Emily, and they stepped away. "Emily, the number one most important ingredient to any relationship is trust. Without it, nothing else can thrive. We're asking you to stay at the auction until the end because Asher wants you here. It's your choice, though. If you believe in Asher, stay. If you don't think you can trust him, leave now and no one will judge you for it."

"That's all you'll tell me?"

"That's all that matters."

ASHER WATCHED HIS father dismiss his brothers and fought against his natural instinct to block Emily's retreat himself. He could have gone to her side, begged or demanded that she not leave, but he could guess what his father was saying, and it struck a chord within him.

If Emily wanted to leave, he would let her go. With her, he would never be the hammer.

Emily held his eyes from across the room and said something to his father then thankfully started walking back toward him. She didn't stop until she was right beside Asher. The buzz of the auction behind them was forgotten as she looked up at him. "In my experience, the people I care about tend to leave me. It's not an excuse, just an explanation. You terrify me."

Asher laced his fingers with hers and said, "You scare the hell out of me, too."

"I don't want us to be over, Asher."

"Then stay." He would have bent to kiss her, but Kenzi gave his upper arm a strong tap.

"Everyone is waiting," she said.

Asher didn't look away from Emily's eyes. "I have to go up to the podium. Come up with me?"

Emily's hand shook in his, but she nodded and allowed herself to be led up to the front of the room. She had a death grip on his hand when everyone's attention turned their way. Asher pried his hand free and slid his arm around her waist. A screen came down behind them and the lights in the room dimmed.

"The last item in the auction comes with a story. It's about a brave woman who came to Boston to tell the owner of a company he couldn't have her land. She had a dream and wouldn't let anyone stand in the way of it." Photos of Emily's grandfather's house being renovated into a museum flashed on the screen behind them. "Some dreams take detours and Emily Harris's did." The next photos were of the houses around her museum being sold off and then of the museum after the fire. She tensed beside him, but he kept going. "By now you know all about the philosophy behind The Harris Tactile Museum, so I'm sure you'll understand why a little thing like a fire shouldn't be allowed to stop something so beautiful from being realized." The next slide was a site plan. "That is why I am donating the Harris Tactile Museum to the town of Welchton. With Emily's permission, the museum will partner with New Hampshire University and become a place that not only celebrates the accomplishments of her and her mother, but also helps others follow in their footsteps. How much do I believe in the philosophy of the Harris Museum?" He looked down into her teary eyes and wiped the tears away with his hands.

"Asher, I had no idea." The wall between them fell away, and everything he'd hoped to see in her eyes was there, and it was so beautiful he wished he could capture it on paper. Her love for him mixed with forgiveness.

He wanted to spend the rest of his days putting that much joy on her face. And he would. He was finally a man who understood not only how to love, but that the love they had for each other was all that really mattered in the end.

He led Emily off to the side of the podium and dropped to one knee. "From the first time I met you I knew I would never be the same. Your perseverance and your dreams inspire me to be a better man. I thought I had everything I wanted until you showed me how much better my life could be with you in it. I want to marry you, Emily Harris. Say yes." He held out a ring.

Emily's eyes filled with tears. She kept looking from the plans on the screen behind the podium to him. "That's why you bought my property?"

He nodded and held his breath. A hush fell over the large audience.

Tears poured down her cheeks and she said, "Yes. Yes. Yes. Yes."

There were cheers and clapping, but Asher didn't look away from Emily. She was all that mattered to him. He stood and slid the ring on her finger. "We'll build it together, Emily. You and I. And it will be something people will travel from all over the world to see."

"And feel," Emily added with a happy, teary smile.

The auctioneer stepped back up to the podium and said, "Profits from the final item will go directly to the Harris Tactile Museum and School of Design fund. Not to set the bar high, but the last donation was half a town. Do I hear ten thousand?"

Asher pulled Emily off the stage, through a door, and into a hallway. As soon as they were alone he kissed her with all his heart, and she kissed him back with all of hers. "If I have to I'll spend the rest of my life earning your trust."

Emily placed a hand on his cheek. "You already have it." She kissed him again deeply, then wrapped her arms around him and hugged him tightly.

Alessandro and Victor approached them and said, "You have some of the steps out of order, but you did good, Asher. You did good."

They kept walking and Emily looked up at Asher. "What are they talking about?"

"I'll explain it to you someday. For now, let's go say our goodbyes and head home. I can't wait to get you alone."

They walked hand in hand toward a door that would lead them into the main hallway. Emily stopped and asked, "When did you know you wanted to marry me?"

Asher pulled her close and kissed her forehead. "You were always mine . . . from the first moment I met you. It just took me a while to figure out what that meant."

Chapter Twenty-One

THE NEXT FEW minutes were a blur of congratulations and hugs. The crowd parted for Sophie and Dale, though. Sophie gave Emily a long hug that would have had Emily bursting into happy tears if Sophie had not said, "Don't you dare cry or you'll have me crying, and I had my makeup professionally done tonight."

"Me, too," Emily said and wiped beneath her eyes. With all the photos being taken she hoped she didn't look like a raccoon.

As if he could read her mind, Asher whispered in her ear, "You look gorgeous."

Dale followed Sophie's hug with one of his own. "Welcome to the family, Emily." He turned to his son and said, "I'm proud of you, Asher. You found your Sophie."

Sophie swatted at him and wiped at her eyes. "Now I'm crying, too. Look what you've done." Despite her reprimand, it was obvious how happy she was with his statement.

Emily glanced at Dale, then Asher, and smiled. When she'd first met Asher she'd thought he was the polar opposite of his parents, but that night she was moved by how similar they were. Asher had proven that he would move heaven and earth for her, just as his father would for his mother. She looked up at Asher and said, "I almost left early, but your father convinced me to stay."

Asher nodded at his father, then stepped away from Emily and surprised everyone by giving Dale a hug. "Thanks, Dad."

Dale closed his eyes for a moment as he hugged his son back. "You're very welcome son. Very welcome."

Celeste joined the group. "Oh, my God. That was the most romantic thing I've ever seen."

Sophie smiled at Celeste. "I agree, and I hope I'm there to see yours."

Wide-eyed, Celeste laughed. "Mine? I'm not even dating anyone."

Sophie looked at Emily and winked. "Yet. I have four more sons."

"Whoa," Celeste said, raising her hands. "I'm not looking to get married."

"Love changes that."

Asher wrapped his arms around Emily again and murmured, "It certainly does." Emily savored the moment. Never in her life had she imagined being this happy or believing that maybe, just maybe, something good could last.

Asher's brothers and Kenzi appeared. Kenzi had a huge smile on her face. "Asher, I didn't know you had it in you, but that was amazing."

Asher smiled and gave his sister a brief hug. "It's like I've always said, you people underestimate me."

Ian shook his head. "Oh, boy. Well, love may have taken his heart, but his ego is intact."

A general chuckle spread through his family.

"Laugh all you want," Asher said, "because Mom is now turning her matchmaking eye at the rest of you."

Sophie smiled in the face of her shocked children's faces. "I'd like grandchildren while I'm young enough to enjoy them. Is that so wrong?"

As the group laughed again, Emily wrapped an arm around Asher's waist. She loved watching him laugh with his family.

My family soon.

She closed her eyes briefly. *Mom, your dream brought me mine. Thank you.*

THAT NIGHT ASHER took Emily to his apartment—their apartment from that night on. He took her coat and although he was excited to finally have her alone, there was something he wanted to show her before he carried her off to his bed. "I have another surprise for you."

"Another one?" Emily's eyes flew to his. "I'm not sure I can take anymore. I'm already so happy I might pass out."

He chuckled and kissed her gently. "Stay conscious. You're going to love this." He looked at the door of his spare bedroom and said, "At least, I hope you will." He turned her around and covered her eyes with his hands. "Now walk."

"So bossy," Emily said with a laugh. "But I love it."

"I'll keep that in mind," he said as images of what they'd do after he gave her the surprise flew through his head. It was difficult to concentrate, but he wanted to do this for Emily. They stopped at the door of the spare bedroom and he said, "No laughing."

She put a hand over his on her eyes. "Oh, did you make something for me? I'm sure I'll love it."

He swung the door open and lowered his hand. Emily gasped and walked inside. What she seemed to notice first was that her own sketches, the ones she'd left in Paris, were framed and hung all around the room. She stopped and touched one of them. It was her sketch of the two of them lying in bed together with their legs and arms entwined, basking in the afterglow of their lovemaking. She threw her arms around him and kissed him so passionately he almost lost control. He broke the kiss off, though, and said, "Did you notice what I added to your collection?"

Emily turned back to take a second look and her head tilted to one side as she took in the framed painting beside her sketch. "You drew stick people."

He took her hand in his and ran it over the painting. "3D stick people."

She looked around the room, a huge smile spreading across her face as one of his sketches caught her attention. "Does that one have a boner?"

He wiggled his eyebrows at her, loving that she was reacting to his gift the way he'd hoped she would. "It does. Do you want to feel it?"

She started laughing softly, then harder and harder until it was impossible not to join her. When she could finally speak, she said, "I love it. I love all of it. And I love you,

Asher. I love your bossy side, your goofy side, your sexy side."

"Wait, I do not have a goofy side. Take that back."

She sidled up to him and grinned. "You drew a stick person with a boner. That's goofy."

He swung her up in his arms. "It was an artist detail that added to the overall ambience of the piece. Besides, you taught me to laugh again, and you'll pay for that."

"Bring it on," Emily said with a sexy laugh. "Bring it on."

Chapter Twenty-Two

A COUPLE DAYS later, Emily was sipping coffee on the couch in the apartment she now shared with Asher when she noticed a package on the table near the door. It was addressed to Asher and felt like a book. She was curious, but she placed it back on the table.

"You can read it if you want," Asher said from behind her.

Emily swung around. "What is it?"

Asher pulled her into his arms and hugged her. "Something the Andrades sent me. I skimmed a few pages, but it's my deceased aunt's journal. I have no desire to read it."

"I might, if you're sure it's okay. I wish my family had kept journals."

Nuzzling her neck, Asher said, "What's mine is yours, at least, as soon as you pick a date."

She went up on her tiptoes to give him a quick kiss on the lips. "I will. I'm looking for the perfect location."

"Pick one soon or I'll pick one for us."

Emily wriggled against him. "I do love it when you talk tough."

"What else do you love?"

Emily ran a hand down his chest, over his flat stomach, and cupped his erection.

"How much time do we have?"

"As much as we need," Asher groaned and claimed her mouth with a kiss that led them back into the bedroom. A while later they were naked and sprawled together on the bed.

Completely at peace with the world, Emily said, "Do you think your family is worried that we haven't surfaced from your apartment yet?"

Asher kissed her bare shoulder. "They'd be more worried if we did. I do need to get back to work, though. Brice is after me for a change. He said—"

Emily rolled onto her back and stretched, and Asher stopped talking. Emily chuckled. "What did he say?"

"Who?"

"Never mind," Emily said and snuggled back up to Asher. Asher's business was waiting for him. A construction company in New Hampshire was waiting to discuss their bid with Emily. Neither mattered in that moment. "Why do bees make terrible friends?"

Asher shook his head. "Why?"

"Because they're always too buzzy to do anything with you."

Asher met Emily's eyes and they both started laughing. "That was awful."

Emily rolled on top of Asher and joked, "You think you can do better?"

He looked up at her seriously and said, "Never. You are my life, Emily, always mine. Don't ever doubt that."

Emily looked up at him and shook her head with a smile. She'd known a love like theirs was possible because she had witnessed it from her grandfather, but she'd never dared hope for it for herself. "If I ever do, I'll look at the painting of you with the boner and—"

He gave her ass a slap. "Remember that it was drawn with love."

Emily laughed and between kisses said, "Yes, that's what I was going to say."

Life was good, but she had a feeling that, with Asher, it would get better and better. Always his? Absolutely.

THE END

Be the first to hear about my releases

ruthcardello.com/signup

One random newsletter subscriber will be chosen every month in 2015. The chosen subscriber will receive a $100 eGift Card! Sign up today by clicking on the link above!

Acknowledgements

I am so grateful to everyone who was part of the process of creating *Always Mine*. Thank you to:

Private Daniel Dubois of the Woonsocket, Rhode Island Fire Department, for helping me decide how and what to burn. And his wife, Kathy Dubois, for joining me on this publishing journey. I am so grateful for all you do.

Nicole Sanders at Trevino Creative Graphic Design for my new cover. You are amazing!

My very patient beta readers. You know who you are. Thank you for kicking my butt when I need it.

My editors: Karen Lawson, Janet Hitchcock, and Marion Archer.

My Roadies for making me smile each day when I log on my computer. So many of you have become friends. Was there life before the Roadies? I'm sure there was, but it wasn't have as much fun.

Thank you to my husband, Tony, who is a saint—simple as that.

Other Books by Ruth

The Legacy Collection:

*Also available in audiobook format

Where my billionaires began.

Book 1: Maid for the Billionaire (available at all major eBook stores for FREE!)

Book 2: For Love or Legacy

Book 3: Bedding the Billionaire

Book 4: Saving the Sheikh

Book 5: Rise of the Billionaire

Book 6: Breaching the Billionaire: Alethea's Redemption

Book 7: A Corisi Christmas Novella

The Andrades

*Also available in audiobook format

A spin off series of the Legacy Collection with cameos from characters you love from that series.

Book 1: Come Away With Me (available at all major eBook stores for FREE!)

Book 2: Home to Me

Book 3: Maximum Risk

Book 4: Somewhere Along the Way

Book 5: Loving Gigi

Recipe For Love, An Andrade Christmas Novella

The Barringtons

A new, seven book series about the Andrade's Boston cousins.

The first series in the Barrington Billionaire WORLD.

Book 1: Always Mine

Book 2: Stolen Kisses (Available for Pre-order)

Book 3: Trade It All (Coming 2016)

Book 4: Let It Burn (Coming 2016)

Book 5: More Than Love (Coming 2016)

Book 6: Forever Now (Coming 2016)

Book 7: Never Goodbye (Coming 2016)

*Look for a linked series set in the same world, written by Jeannette Winters (my sister).

You won't have to read her series to enjoy mine, but it sure will make it more fun. Characters will appear in both series.

Author Jeannette Winters

Book 1: One White Lie (Coming late 2015)

Book 2: Table for Two

Book 3: You & Me Make Three

Book 4: Virgin for the Fourth Time

Book 5: His for Five Nights

Book 6: After Six

My characters also appear in her Betting on You Series in the Billionaire's Longshot.

Book 1: The Billionaire's Secret (FREE!)

Book 2: The Billionaire's Masquerade

Book 3: The Billionaire's Longshot

Book 4: The Billionaire's Jackpot

Novella: All Bets Off

Lone Star Burn Series:

Fun, hot romances that roam from the country to the city and back.

Book 1: Taken, Not Spurred

Book 2: Tycoon Takedown

Book 3: (Coming soon)

The Temptation Series:

Guaranteed to put you on Santa's naughty list.

Twelve Days of Temptation and Be My Temptation
Two hot novellas about one sizzling couple.

Other Books:

Taken By a Trillionaire

Ruth Cardello, JS Scott, Melody Anne.

Three hot fantasies about alpha princes and the women who tame them.

Author Biography

Ruth Cardello was born the youngest of 11 children in a small city in northern Rhode Island. She spent her young adult years moving as far away as she could from her large extended family. She lived in Boston, Paris, Orlando, New York—then came full circle and moved back to Rhode Island. She now happily lives one town over from the one she was born in. For her, family trumped the warmer weather and international scene.

She was an educator for 20 years, the last 11 as a kindergarten teacher. When her school district began cutting jobs, Ruth turned a serious eye toward her second love– writing and has never been happier. When she's not writing, you can find her chasing her children around her small farm, riding her horses, or connecting with her readers online.

Contact Ruth:
Website: RuthCardello.com
Email: Minouri@aol.com
FaceBook: Author Ruth Cardello
Twitter: @RuthieCardello